CAVE CRAWLERS

ALEX LAYBOURNE

SEVERED PRESS
HOBART TASMANIA

CAVE CRAWLERS

CHAPTER ONE

June 1984

Declan Howland looked down at the ground beneath him. His arms shook as he held his weight and tried to reposition his feet.

Sweat stung his eyes, and his jaw hurt, it was clenched so hard. Scrambling, kicking at the tree as if hoping he could create a foothold in its trunk, Declan realized that it was no use. He had made a stupid mistake, trying to climb too fast. For what? Just so his mother wouldn't see what he was up to?

Declan could hear his brother playing back closer to the house. Two years younger than him, Justin was a quiet and most definitely a geek, but Declan loved him.

His fingers slipped, losing their grip on the tree branch, a moment of panic surged through his young body. Everything slowed down, from his fingers slipping one by one, to the moment of weightlessness, where he hung in the air, three meters up, and but a few centimeters too short.

Declan knew the impact was coming and tried to brace himself for it, but before he had the chance, time caught up with him and he was hurtling towards the ground. The rain from the day before meant the grass was wet, cushioning his fall to a small degree. It just wasn't enough to stop the bone in his left arm from snapping as a result of the impact.

The air rushed out of his lungs, momentarily silencing his screams. That changed, however, the moment he tried to turn and get back to his feet. As soon as he applied pressure to his left arm, a shooting pain surged through his body, overloading his brain with a burst of agony so hot that even Declan could not stop from crying out.

He closed his eyes, hoping the sound didn't travel to the house.

"Declan?" He heard his brother calling his name, worry heavy in his voice.

Declan wanted to shout to him, to tell him to stay away, but it was too late.

1

"Declan, are you okay?" Justin hurried to his brother, dropping into the wet ground beside him.

Declan opened his eyes and looked up at his brother's worried face, the round eyes wide with the constant stream of questions that always seemed to be flowing. His curly brown hair was wild and unruly from rolling around in the grass with this Action Man toys. Behind him, he saw the blue sky with subtle wisps of cloud feathering the view.

"Justin, get —" he couldn't finish the sentence for he was cut off by the alarmed cry and heavy gait of his mother, who was approaching the two boys at full speed.

"What on earth has happened here?" Peggy Howland asked, her voice not asking, but accusing, the course of events already created in her mind. "What did you do?"

As always, her eyes turned towards her youngest son.

Justin looked up at his mother, terror evident on his face, as the blood drained from his cheeks and the realization of what was to come hit him.

"Nothing, Mama," Justin said, backing away. Even at the age of ten, Justin knew enough to understand when he was cornered. When to fight, when to run, and when to stay quiet.

The only problem was that for Justin, none of the approaches ever seemed to offer a different outcome.

"I fell, Mama," Declan said from the floor.

He held his injured arm, cradling it with his right as if it were a sling. Pain brought tears to his eyes, but he would not let them fall. The emotion was not something that was shown in front of the adults in the Howland household. It was kept and stored away for after lights out, where the pillows of duvets could stifle the boys' cries.

"What have I told you about lying, Declan, honey?" Peggy asked, crouching down to stroke her son's hair across his sweat-soaked forehead. Yet even as she did so, her gaze never left Justin.

The younger brother was frozen. Caught in the headlights, he had nowhere to run.

"I'm not lying, Mama. I was climbing the tree, and I fell." Declan stared up at the tree branch he had been so desperate to reach.

"It's alright, baby," she whispered, rising from her crouched position on the floor.

'Mama, no," Declan cried out, as his mother walked away.

"Quiet now, baby," Peggy replied as she bored down on Justin, who stumbled backward, whimpering.

"I didn't, Mama, I was playing —" Justin stammered.

"Liar, you pushed him, didn't you?" Peggy screamed, raising her hand.

"Mama, I fell, please, don't hurt him," Declan cried out, trying to force himself to his feet, but the pain in his arm sent him crashing back into the wet ground.

Peggy flung out her arm, the back out of hand catching Justin across the side of his head, knocking him to the floor, where he lay crying.

"Mama, please, I didn't do anything. I didn't even see. I was playing Action Man," Justin pleaded, pointing from the floor to the second-hand toys that were scattered through the garden.

Peggy stood over her youngest son, her nostrils flared, and her face flushed with rage. "Just you wait until your father gets home."

Turning, she helped Declan to his feet and hurried him back into the house. The whole way, Declan had his head turned back, looking at his brother, the afternoon sun glinting on the trail of tears that streaked his cheeks.

Justin remained on the floor, his head throbbed from the impact of the blow, and he was scared to stand in case his mother saw him and came back to vent her wrath some more. The wet grass was cool against his burning cheeks. Digging his fingers into the soft earth beneath him, Justin wished the ground would open and swallow him. Anything would be better than what he knew lay in store for him. It was only when he heard the growl of his mother's Volvo roar from inside the garage that Justin found the strength to get to his feet.

He walked slowly, his body shaking with a cold that was driven by the fear that stood beside him, stroking the back of his neck, making him shudder, Justin gathered his toys from the garden and took them inside.

The house seemed that much larger when he was left on his own. When he was younger, it scared him, but now, he had learned to relish the space and the silence of the house. He could move freely, without counting the steps to avoid the three that creaked. He didn't have to tiptoe past his father's study, although even alone, he would never dare open to door or go inside.

Once he had his toys tidied away, he looked at the TV and considered setting on the cartoons, but there was work to be done still.

With a sigh, he went to the kitchen and started doing the dishes. The radio was on, and Michael Jackson was singing his new single, Thriller. The music made Justin dance as he washed, careful not to get any suds on the floor.

As Michael finished, another band came on that Justin liked. He had seen them on the TV a few weeks before, and his dad had caught him watching it. He called him a faggot and sent him to his room without dinner. Justin didn't understand. He liked the song; it was catchy. Music helped to take his mind away from the house and the world around him. It distracted him, which was normally a good thing, sweeping him along like a waking dream.

It came as quite a surprise, therefore, when the music suddenly ended and plunged the house into near silence. The only sound was the gentle fizz of the remaining suds in the sink, and the tap, tap, tap of a foot on the linoleum floor.

A voice in Justin's mind told him not to turn around, but he knew he had no choice. His father stood in the doorway, his arms folded, his mechanics overalls stained with grease and oil. His father owned his own garage in town and always smelled of motor oil. It didn't matter if he was home for lunch, fresh out of the shower, or heading to church on a Sunday morning, he always smelled like a car engine.

"H … Hi, Dad," Justin stammered, trying but failing to hide his surprise.

"Where's your mother?" he asked, his voice more of a growl. He strode across the kitchen, heading to the fridge. He wrenched open the door and pulled out a six-pack of beer. He yanked two cans out of the holders. Opening one, he downed half the can and gave a long, loud belch. "I asked you a question."

"She … she had to take Declan to the hospital. He fell, fell from the tree," Justin whimpered. He didn't want to step off the booster step he used to reach the sink, but he had to.

Doing so made him feel even smaller, especially as his father bore down on him. A tall man by any measure, his father cut an imposing figure.

"Oh, that's not good. I hope he didn't break anything," Jackson Howland said, almost as if speaking to himself.

"How did he fall?" Jackson asked, his eyes focusing on Justin.

"I didn't see, Daddy. I was playing in the grass. He said he was climbing and just fell." Justin backed up as his father took a long step closer to him.

Justin tried to swallow, but his mouth was dry. His heart thundered in his chest as he stared into the eyes of something he didn't understand. Parents were supposed to love their children, but Justin feared his beyond any ability to describe. He didn't know if there was a word for it, for the way his father looked at him, or for the anger he let control him, but if there was, Justin would have used it to describe his life.

"That must have been frightening to see him like that, right?" Jackson said, finishing the beer and throwing the empty can into the sink, where it crashed into the remaining soap suds.

"Yes, Daddy." Justin didn't understand the question and didn't know if he was supposed to say yes or no, but silence was an even worse choice.

"Well, I'm sure the doctors will fix him. Come here." Jackson dropped to his knees and held his arms open for Justin to slide into his embrace.

Hesitant, Justin took small, uncertain steps, his shoes squeaking on the floor. He approached his father, who stood patiently waiting. Then, like the Venus flytrap his brother kept on the window sill in his bedroom, his arms closed, and he was trapped in their strong embrace.

"You lying little shit," Jackson growled. "If you hurt that boy in any way, then there will be hell to pay."

Jackson was fast, switching his weight, he thrust his left leg out, placing his foot on the floor, his knee bent at ninety degrees.

"Daddy, no, I didn't hurt him. He fell," Justin said, struggling against his father's grip. It was an impossible task, he knew that, but the desire to survive and escape the pain that he knew was coming always brought out the fight in him.

Jackson released his grip on his son momentarily, in order to get a better hold. He grabbed Justin by the wrist, twisting it behind his back, pushing it higher and higher until Justin screamed in pain. The pressure was enough to lead Justin like a dog on a leash, he pulled him over his knee, controlling him with one hand, while the other grabbed the drying towel from the kitchen side.

"I ain't got a belt, so this will have to do, you disrespectful bastard," Jackson roared.

"Daddy, please, no, no, Daddy." Justin squirmed as his father yanked his trousers down to his knees, exposing his rear end and genitals to the cool kitchen air.

"Shut up, and take what's coming to you. Be a man, for once." Jackson lost himself in the rage that haunted him, controlling his actions as if he were a junkie and the high of rage was the only thing that could help keep him sane.

The first strike from the towel stung, but Justin kept his mouth shut, biting down on his lip to keep from screaming.

The second and third began to burn, and after that, the pain just flared, rising up like a fire, swallowing more and more of him with each strike.

Justin lost count of how many times his father whipped him with the cloth, but he stopped after a time to twirl the towel into a much finer instrument.

By the time it was over, Jackson was panting and Justin was crying; his body burned and he could barely feel anything. The copper taste of blood filled his mouth from where he had bitten his lip so hard he broke the skin.

Jackson pushed his son off of him and stood up. Staring down at his half-naked son, he opened the second beer and gave a grunt of disappointment. "Get to your room, I'm done with you." Turning, he stalked his way across the kitchen and into the living room.

Lost in the inferno that raged within him, Justin remained where he was. Rolling onto his back, the cool floor soothed his flesh. He knew he needed to get going. If his dad came back for another beer and found him in the kitchen still, then it wouldn't end well for him.

He moved with a heavy limp, using every ounce of strength he had left to support himself, Justin pulled himself to the stairs and up into his room.

Justin barely had the strength to crawl under the bed covers, he curled himself into as tight of a ball as his body would allow, cocooned himself within the duvet, and let the tears take him away.

Justin didn't know if he slept, or how many hours passed, but he finally heart Declan come into the room, closing the door behind him.

Justin tried to keep still, but his body ached, and even the slightest movement brought a whimper from him. He had grown deaf to them, but in the silence of the room, there would be no mistaking it.

"Justin?" Declan asked, his voice gentle.

Justin gave no answer, so Declan climbed onto the bed and put his arm over the ball of blankets and boy. "It's going to be alright, Justin. I'm going to look after you."

The embrace was separated by the blanket, but Justin felt the warmth nonetheless. It brought a fresh wave of tears to his eyes and shudder to his breaths. "Why?" Justin didn't understand. Declan had an easy ride; he never got into trouble.

"Because that's why big brothers are for," Declan said, laying his head on the pillow. The boys drifted off to sleep, as they often did, only with each other for comfort and a desperation for any kind of slumber, for even the worst nightmare would be a joy compared to the one they lived every day.

CHAPTER TWO

Declan's cast ran from around his thumb up to his elbow. It was a creamy color and hard as a rock. Justin had been all too pleased when Declan said he was allowed to draw on it.

"Go on, it was the doctor's orders," Declan said as Justin's hands trembled, just short of making contact with the cast.

"What if they don't like it?" Justin asked, his voice timid and shy.

"It will be fine, trust me." Declan smiled, and Justin felt better. He drew a pair of figures. One him and the other his brother. They were smiling happy boys, a football drawn suspended in the air between them.

The picture was a lie. They never got to smile too much, and throwing a ball would never be tolerated.

"Sorry we couldn't go to the pool," Declan said a few hours later as they sat in the garden, beneath the shade of the same tree Declan had tried to scale.

"It's okay. I like hanging with you." Justin looked up at his brother and smiled, before returning his attention to the card he held in his hand. It depicted a 1967 Chevy Impala, and while Justin didn't know the meaning of the different statistics listed on the bottom of the card, he sure knew which one he was going to use. "Quarter mile, seventeen seconds."

"Dang, you win again," Declan said, handing over his card before fisting the air as he saw the next card in his deck.

The boys would spend hours playing Top Trump. They had three decks between them. Two were full, while the muscle cars one was missing two cards. However, that was their favorite deck, so they often played it anyway.

"Justin Howland, what do you think you are doing? Sitting there playing games while there is work to be done. The dishes won't just clean themselves you know, and the vacuuming needs doing also." Peggy stormed halfway down the garden, allowing her squawking voice to carry the rest of the way.

"I did the dishes last night," Justin whined; an act he regretted almost instantly.

"Don't take that tone with me, young man. Your brother is injured. He can't do anything, so march inside right now and get those chores finished."

Justin got up from the ground and brushed himself down. "Yes, Mama," he said, letting his head hang low as he walked towards his mother's impatient figure.

"You are getting worse by the day," she growled as she turned and moved back towards the house.

"It's not fair, I want to play with Declan," Justin couldn't help but complain.

"That's just it. You want to play, but laziness is a sign of the devil. You are a lazy little boy, and nothing good happens to lazy people," Peggy snarled, picking up her pace.

"I'm not lazy, Mama, I just want to play outside. Please let me stay outside, please." Peggy stopped walking and spun around to face her son, who had stopped walking and stood with a child's defiance on his face.

"You want to stay outside?" Peggy moved towards him. "Really, you want to stay out here?"

Justin backed up a couple of steps as the sudden realization of what his mother meant dawned on him.

"No, Mama. I'll come inside and clean up." Justin backed up another step, as his mother refused to slow down or change the direction of her movement.

Peggy lashed out, grabbed Justin by the wrist and pulled him to her.

"Mama, no," Justin screamed, panic consuming him. "Mama, not that, please. No! No!" Justin fought against his mother's grip, but there was no use. The grip was not to be broken, and Justin was dragged across the garden to the shed. The small wooden shed was dark and dank. Justin hated it. That was where the spiders lived.

"You wanted to stay outside, so here you go, stay outside." Peggy forced her son into the shed and slammed the door shut, only missing Justin's fingers by a few millimeters.

The darkness was not quite total, as the gaps in the wooden panels that formed the walls of the shed let slices of light through in various quantities. Not that it provided any comfort, for all it did was create even more shadows that danced around Justin's head.

Justin turned around, pressing his back against the door, he faced the shed. He jumped as a ray of sunlight glinted on the eyes of a monster that lay curled up in the far corner of the shed. White eyes gazed at him, and Justin was sure he could hear the raspy breaths of a nightmare creature as it woke. Shaking his head, he looked again. The light was not from a monster, but rather a reflection from two paint cans that had fallen over the shelf unit that ran along the rear wall.

Justin closed his eyes, trying to wash away the images his brain insisted on creating, but that only made it worse. He felt something tickle the back of his arm. Legs. He could feel them scurrying along his flesh as the spiders marched over him.

Justin slapped angrily at his body, imagining hundreds of spiders, their thick black legs as wide as his fingers and as hairy as his gran's chin, crawling all over him, on his bare arms and beneath his shirt. He slapped himself until it hurt, but nothing could convince him that he was not still covered with the creatures. No matter how hard he fought, he could not hold off the sensation of the creeping, crawling bugs from his skin. Justin's heart rate skyrocketed, and his breathing increased to match. He felt dizzy as a strange spreading warmth ran through his body, and then, with a rush like a wave crashing on the beach, the true blackness came.

Justin collapsed to the floor, crashing into the junk that had been thrown into the shed over the years. Only then, when his unconscious form became just another addition to the floor, did the first spider come out of hiding and explore the newest addition.

Declan waited for his mother to disappear into the kitchen before he made his way over to the shed. He waited for the music to start, and that was when he opened the door. Declan never understood why his parents treat him and his brother so differently. He had asked, but they simply punished Justin for being a tattler.

His hands shook as he worked the padlock from the door. Declan took a deep breath as he peered inside. Justin was lying on his side, his body covered in spiders, at least a dozen, the majority nothing but the big shed spiders; tiny bodies with long gangly legs, but there were several garden spiders, their striped bodies fat like soaked raisins. Black legs prodded at the podgy skin of Justin's cheek. Declan hated spiders, but he loved his brother so he brushed them all off, slapping at them until his body was clean. He moved into a crouch, and grabbed his brother by the shoulders. Declan heaved him out of the shed, grunting with the effort it took to do so with just one arm. Justin woke up as he was halfway out of the door and was able to help push himself free.

Declan pulled his brother to the side of the house and held him, cradling him like a protector. "It's going to be alright, Justin. I promise."

Justin couldn't find the strength to speak. His body shook with cold and his teeth chattered every time he relaxed his jaw. Instead, he sought comfort in his brother's embrace, but found a sadness there, because he knew it would not always last.

However, it was what they had, and in each other, they had a bond that could not be broken. Both understood that the life they lived was not like the life of anybody else they knew, but at the same time, it was their life, and to wish it away still felt wrong somehow.

"How about we go up to our room and play a game of Monopoly or something?" Declan offered as his brother's sobs died down.

"You hate Monopoly." Justin looked up at his brother. He felt ashamed, and he felt angry. A range of emotions that he could not quite put words to bubbled within him.

"No, but you like it, so what do you say?" Declan knew his brother wouldn't able to resist a chance to play the world's most boring and never-ending game.

"Can I be the battleship?"

"You can be anything you want."

"Cool, then let's go." Justin got to his feet and froze.

To get inside and into the bedroom would mean going past their mother. Unless they went around the side and in through the front door, but that was usually locked when their father wasn't home.

"Don't worry, she's listening to her tunes; she won't even notice," Declan whispered. "You go upstairs and I'll get us both a drink and something to snack on."

Justin held his breath as he crept through the kitchen. Peggy didn't notice, however. She was lost to her music and a cigarette, the cloud from which hung in the kitchen, gathering above her head like a brooding storm.

The house they lived in was a decent size, and while there was a spare guest room that was never used, the boys were made to share. They liked it that way too.

Their room was decorated with a simple blue and white striped wallpaper and a dark blue carpet. Their beds, which were bunk beds until a few weeks before, stood on opposite sides of the room. A large window occupied the wall between the two items of furniture, while a toy chest stood beneath it, guarding their more valuable toys. The board games were in the closet, and while Justin had grown a lot over the last year, almost catching up with his brother, he still couldn't quite reach the shelf where they sat.

So he sat on the floor and watched as Declan pulled down several boxes of games, including Monopoly. He had brought a bag of chips from the kitchen, and two cans of cola for them to drink. Their bedroom was their sanctuary, and for some reason, it was the one place in the house their parents rarely entered and always behaved in. Justin found a great comfort in the room and was always happy when Declan suggested they stay there to play.

The afternoon moved by with them moving through four different board games and the entire bag of chips. By the time their father got home, they had forgotten the problems of the morning and were even looking forward to the smells coming up from the kitchen, of the meal their mother was cooking.

CHAPTER THREE

May 1992

The rain hammered against the windows, but the horizon was starting to brighten, a shimmering possibility that the three days of rain were finally over and a dry spell was looming.

Justin was sitting in his room, headphones over his ears, the Walkman he had worked to save for was playing Guns N' Roses November Rain. It wasn't his favorite song, but it was a mixtape he had made from the radio, and any music would help to distract him from the world around him.

He sat at the desk, in the gloom of his room, only the desk lamp providing any sort of light on the large piece of paper that was spread over the desktop.

A collection of pencils laid spread around the image that Justin was working on. Still in its early outlining phase, he was working on the main focal character, a superhero of his own creation, leaning heavily on the DC characters he enjoyed reading so much.

Justin had been twelve when he first discovered comics, and once he had his own bedroom, he started collecting them with the money he earned on his paper route, and then, as he got older, from the wages he was paid for working at the local grocery store. Mr. Bukowski was a nice man who had three children, all of them a lot old than Justin was. Justin had never met them, but he guessed they were in their twenties or thirties, given how old Mr. Bukowski looked.

Justin worked weekends and three evenings a week at the grocery store, and he loved every minute of it, being out of the house, talking to people. He picked up every shift he could take, as long as it didn't interfere with his schoolwork. He did it for the money too. While it didn't pay a lot, and even less after he bought comics and the meager art supplies he needed, Justin had still managed to save up a decent sum of money. As soon as he was old enough, Justin was moving on.

Top of his class in school, he was looking forward to going to a university to study design. He had dreams of becoming an illustrator.

When he wasn't at work or at school, Justin was in his room, rarely coming out to interact with his family, other than his brother. He would draw image after image, sometimes large murals on rolls of paper, other times small scenes sketched onto some sticky notes. He loved the place his mind would take him to when he started drawing and was more than happy to spend his free time there … anything to take him away from the depressing place in which he lived.

He didn't hear the door to his room open, not the sound of his name being called. The first time he realized he was not alone was when the hand fell on his shoulder, causing him to jump out of his seat.

"Declan, Jesus, you made me piss myself," Justin said, slapping at his brother's arm. "Don't creep up on a guy like that."

"Sorry, I called you, but you weren't listening, as usual." Declan placed an extra flare of sarcasm on the words as he looked over his brother's shoulder at the current work in progress. "Looking good. What's it going to be this time?"

Justin looked back at the piece of art and took a slow breath. "I'm not sure yet." There were outlines of a building, a tenement block most likely, and several others on a street lined with cars. The superhero character was off to one side, watching down the street at whatever was going on.

"I'm going to guess a building fire. Someone set fire to apartment blocks, maybe a fight between mob families. Your hero is there to rescue some cute damsel in distress," Declan said, pointing at the outlined of the building. "She's right behind that window there."

Justin rolled his eyes. "It's always about the damsels in distress with you."

"Damn right it is; they are always grateful, if you know what I mean." Declan gave a wink and then started laughing.

"Ugh, that might wash with your friends, but you can't fool me, brother." Justin returned the smile and half turned back to his drawing. "What did you want anyway?"

"I wanted to ask if I could borrow the car. We are heading to the movies and I want to pick Annie up in it tonight. That way we can have some alone time, once the movie is finished," Declan said, kissing the air with big wet smooches.

"But I have to work tonight," Justin began to complain.

"Oh, well what time?" Declan asked, his head already thinking ahead of possible options.

"I start at five, but need to get some things first, so wanted to leave at four," Justin answered, pausing. "I'll tell you what. If it's dry when I leave, you can have the car and I'll go on the bike."

"You mean that?" Declan asked, his mood suddenly improved.

"Yep, now get out of here, I want to get some more of this done before I leave." Justin ushered his brother out of the door and replaced the headphones over his ears. November Rain had stopped, much like the rain outside his window was doing, and instead Duran, Duran was warbling some ballad that Justin just could never get into.

Justin returned to his drawing, picking up his pencil, and losing himself his art. Before he knew it, he had the first tendrils of smoke rising from the damsel's window creeping up the page. The flames themselves would have to wait, however, because when he next looked at his watch, it was time to get ready for work.

Dressed and ready for work, Justin stopped by his brother's room, where he threw the car keys onto the desk. Declan sat hunched over his desk, working on an English essay that was no doubt overdue, or on its final deadline extension.

"You will probably need to put some gas in it, depending on what movie house you are going to," Justin said as his brother looked around.

"Okay, cool. Thanks, bro." Declan smiled.

"Hey, that's what little brothers are for, right?" Justin returned the smile and left.

His parents were both at home, his dad sitting in the living room, his ass parked in the large chair positioned right before the TV, a can of beer in hand and several empties lying on the floor by his feet. His mother was in the kitchen, prepping a dinner that she seemed to have forgotten neither child would be there to eat.

"Where are you going?" his dad growled, just happening to look up as Justin passed through the open door.

"Work," Justin answered, not wanting to expel any more air on his old man than was truly necessary.

"When will you be back?" his mother asked from the kitchen.

"I'm working til close, and taking my bike, so not until late," he answered, putting his jacket on as he spoke.

"Oh, well, then you will need to fix yourself something to eat because this meal won't keep." Peggy turned her back and disappeared deeper into the kitchen, her piece spoken.

Justin didn't bother giving an answer. He didn't care enough to do so. Instead, he grabbed his bike key, and backpack from by the front door, and was gone, pedaling down Clarence Street in the direction of town. He needed to drop by the art store and see if the watercolors and market pens he'd ordered had arrived yet.

Declan watched his younger brother leave the house, happy to see him get away without any trouble. As the years went by, Declan had tried to do everything he could to rationalize his parent's behavior. From thinking that he was the problem, that it was his fault they treated him so differently, to blaming Justin for it, convincing himself that his brother was asking for the problems because of his attitude. However, none of that was true, and now, as he stood on the cusp of manhood, with the prospect of moving out looming large on the horizon, he realized that it wasn't their fault at all. It was his parents. They were the only ones to blame, and he and his brother had been conditioned to accept that sort of behavior as normal.

Declan was waiting for a promotion at work, one that would see him become a sort of manager within the frozen vegetable factory where he worked. Once that came through, he would finally be able to move out, and he planned on taking his brother with him, away from their family, away from the dangers that were always bubbling beneath the surface.

After he had showered and changed his clothes, Declan grabbed his wallet and took a few of the bills he had stored away in his lock box. He only ever kept a certain amount of cash for spending, while the rest went into his savings account. Taking enough to make sure he could show Annie Wallace a good time, he splashed on some cologne and hurried downstairs.

"Honey, do you want some dinner?" Peggy asked as she heard her son's footsteps on the stairs.

"No, I'm going out with some friends. We're grabbing a pizza and a movie," Declan answered as he grabbed his jacket and slid the car keys into his pocket.

"Oh, well, I'll plate you up a meal anyway. You can eat it when you get home." Peggy didn't wait for a response but moved the already-plated meal to the kitchen side where it could cool off before she covered it and placed it in the fridge.

"Alright," Declan said under his breath, opening the door and pulling it closed without looking back.

The car was parked on the street. The older model Ford had a small oil leak and his father did not want them parking it in the driveway.

The car started on the first try, and without so much as a cough, Declan pulled away. He slid a cassette into the player, and Iron Maiden began to blast through the speakers. Declan didn't know if Annie was a metal fan, but she would be by the time he was finished. He had a range of cassettes and would take her through it in stages.

Justin didn't mind giving up the car to his brother. He enjoyed being out on the bike. The rush of fresh air helped him clear his mind, and let go of the problems and heavy thoughts that haunted him most hours of the day. It also meant that he would be home later, and that was a fine thing in his book.

With the prospect of university looming, provided he got accepted, Justin knew that he was getting close to the end. He had survived hell and more pain than any child deserved to know about. He felt bad for his parents, that they had no other capabilities than to resort to abuse. It didn't mean he loved them or felt anything for them, but he refused to lower to their level, as that would, in his mind, only validate their choices.

Horn Hill was a small town, a satellite of a larger city. They picked up on a lot of passing trade, but very few people stayed long enough to really look around. The grocery store was located on the edges, picking up those as they arrived, or left, depending on what direction they were traveling.

It was not one of the large chain supermarkets, of which the town somehow had two of, but it did enough business to survive, and for Justin, that was the main thing. He knew everything about surviving. That was part of what drew him to the Help Wanted sign that had been placed in the window.

The shop was empty when he walked in and was likely to never have more than a handful of people in at any one time. It was calm, and it was easy going, and for Justin, it was a little slice of heaven.

It was almost ten and closing time was fast approaching. There had not been a customer for almost an hour, so Justin locked the register and went to start stocking shelves. He was done with the tomato soup, about ready to swap out an empty tray of minestrone, when he heard the door close.

Rising from the crouch he had been in, he saw two figures walking along the window towards cooling units at the back of the shop.

Justin moved the box of soups against the side of the aisle, and returned to the register where he waited for the customers to return.

Justin recognized the pair from school. Both were girls he shared some classes with. Popular with the jocks, Cassie Martin and Sarah-Jayne Hudson were both good-looking girls. Not the sort of people Justin mixed with. He stuck more to himself at school. He couldn't let anybody get close.

"Don't I know you from somewhere?" Sarah-Jayne asked, as she loudly chewed on a piece of gum.

"English class," Cassie replied without skipping a beat.

"That's right," Justin answered, smiling.

"I remember the presentation you gave on that Orwell book, Animal Farm," Cassie continued, her eyes locking onto Justin's, which caused him to feel a rush of excitement and an equally powerful rush of fear tear through his body.

"Thank you," Justin said, not sure how to respond.

"I didn't know you worked here," Cassie said, taking control of the conversation, something that did not seem to bother Sarah-Jayne who was already being distracted by the gossip magazines that lined the front of the register counter.

"Yeah, I've been working for about a year, I guess. It's easy going, the hours are flexible for school, and it helps me earn a bit," Justin said, stumbling his way through the conversation.

"Well, we need to get going, but I'm sure I'll be back again." Cassie smiled, and Justin felt something inside of him melt. Or rather, he felt something that had long ago been broken was now fusing back together again.

Justin watched the girls leave, and felt a little giddy for a time after they left. He forgot about the soup cans, and instead stood by the register, lost in thought. It was fifteen minutes after the scheduled closing time that he finally snapped back into the real world, locked up the shop, and finished tidying away the items he had started to unpack.

It was pushing midnight by the time he got home, locking his bike away just as the lights of the car he shared with Declan pulled into the street.

He stood outside and waited for his brother. He watched the car pull into the street, and park almost in line with the curb. The engine idled for a while before Declan shut it off and stumbled out of the car. While not blind drunk, it was clear that he had had a few too many. Walking over to help him, Justin shook his head at his brother.

"You need to be careful drinking and driving. They are cracking down on that sort of thing." Justin helped his brother to the door, where he sat down on the small porch step and pulled a cigarette out of his coat pocket.

"I know, bro, I know. But it was worth it," Declan said with a drunken smile. He put the cigarette between his lips, lit it, and took a deep drag.

"I didn't know you smoked." Justin looked at his brother.

"I don't. Not really. Just a couple when I have a drink. Makes it all taste way better." Declan giggled and took another drag.

The brothers sat side by side, watching the night roll in. At some point, the church bell rang, a distant sound, signaling the arrival of the midnight hour. The world was quiet save for the tolling of the bell, and Justin felt as if could live in that quiet forever. Then his mind conjured up images of Cassie Martin, and his perspective changed.

Holding his tongue, not wanting to say anything stupid to his big brother, for while they shared a bond formed in the fires of suffering and abuse, a big brother remained such, and any opportunity away from home to tease a younger sibling could not be passed up.

"Let's get to bed, I'm knackered," Declan announced, pushing himself to his feet and flicking the third cigarette butt of their conversation to the floor.

Justin followed his brother inside, careful not to make any noise, moving slowly, closing the door, holding the latch to save it from clicking, a sound his father had claimed woke him on several occasions. He crept through the house, not needing the light to help guide him through the room, evading the furniture scattered about the living room, Justin followed his brother upstairs. While he was only a minute or two behind him, Declan was already snoring by the time Justin walked past his brother's room on route to his own.

***

Declan woke with a jolt. Sunlight was streaming through the windows, and his head had a gentle ache. He could remember most things about the evening, including the fun he'd had with Annie, first in the back of the theatre, and then again once they ditched the others.

Another crashing sound, similar to that which had ripped him from sleep came from downstairs.

Declan was up on his feet in an instant, grabbing a pair of jeans flung over his desk chair, and was out of the door. He knew the sound of a fight when it was brewing in the house. He just hoped he wasn't too late to stop things.

"You lying little shit. Don't you lie to me," Jackson Howland roared as he slammed his youngest son against the wall. His giant fists held Justin's shirt in two large bunches, pulling it up and above his navel.

"I'm not lying," Justin stammered, the tears flowing down his cheeks.

"No, of course fucking not. They just got there as if by magic," Jackson spat, pulling his son away from the wall only to hurl him back into it again.

Justin groaned as the back of his head hit the living room wall, and for a moment, his world started to spin. He could feel his father's rage pulsing deep within him, traveling through his arms like a wave, and jumping into Justin's body.

"I don't know how they got there, but I know they are not mine." Justin had to force the words out as his father's grip was also crushing his chest, making it hard to breathe.

"Bullshit. I can smell them on you. You fucking stink of those cancer sticks. You want to get cancer fine, but don't you dare sully my house with their stench or your discarded junk." Thick strands of spit flew from Jackson's lips, covering Justin's face. The old man's eyes bulged in his head and the skin of his face and neck had turned a deep red shade, as the rage pressure continued to build.

"They were mine," Declan shouted before his father had the chance to go any further with his abuse. "I smoked them."

Jackson's grip lessened slightly. Not letting Justin go, but releasing him enough so that he could breathe once more.

"You don't need to lie for him anymore, son. This cancerous bastard isn't worth the trouble." Jackson looked at his eldest son to his youngest, his face scrunched up by hard years and hard booze, like that of a gargoyle etched into the stones of a cathedral.

"I'm not lying, Dad. They were mine," Declan insisted, stepping forward towards the pair, reaching out with a trembling hand. While until now he had escaped all forms of wrath or abuse from his parents, the question was always lingering in the back of his mind. *When will it be my turn?*

Jackson took several deep, angry breaths, like a bull stuck in the stall, just waiting to be given the signal to raise merry hell.

"Listen to your father," Peggy spoke up, appearing from the hallway, a tea towel in her hands. "Your brother needs to learn the rules. They are simple, and breaking them means punishment."

Declan stepped back and looked at both his parents, in turn, the depths of their craziness becoming more and more evident to him. He opened his mouth to speak, but his mother beat him to it.

"Go on upstairs, let us deal with this. You're both adults now, so it is time to learn to accept the consequences of your actions." Peggy moved forward, standing between her sons, the cloth in her hand taut, as if ready to be used as a weapon at the slightest provocation.

Declan refused to move, but his mother was even more resilient. As his father turned his attention back to Justin, Peggy made her move, grabbing Declan by the arm and pulling him away, pushing him first into the hall, and then over to the stairs.

"Go upstairs now, before you need disciplining too." It was the first time so much as a threat had been cast in his direction, and it chilled Declan to the marrow in his bones.

Declan hadn't even reached halfway when he heard Justin cry out.

"Don't you try and get physical with me, you ungrateful cunt," Jackson's voice boomed from within the living room, as a heavy thud followed swiftly thereafter.

Declan stopped and pivoted on the stairs, but his mother was still standing at the base, her face impassive, her arms folded over each other.

Once in his room, Declan kicked out at the desk chair, pain radiating through his body as his big toe bore the brunt of his frustration. He heard the cries coming from downstairs, and he sank to the floor beside his bed, placing his hands over his ears, hoping he could drown out the sound. His mind played him visions of the time his father had gotten drunk and beat Justin just because they were out of beer. The lashes he had given had cut through the flesh of Justin's ass cheeks. It took almost a week before he left his room, the beating so severe it left him unable to walk or lay any other way than on his belly.

Declan started to cry as his father's rage reached it's most brutal. He heard his brother scream even above the sound of his thundering heart and bellowing memories.

Closing his eyes, Declan pressed his hands to his ears, pushing so hard his forearms ached and his head started to hurt, all the while the screams of his brother echoed through his mind along with his father's incessant voice.

Worthless cunt! Ungrateful bastard, loser, faggot.

The sounds grew and grew until they blended into a tumultuous din, where no one word or turn of phrase could be separated from the other.

Declan swayed backward and forwards on the floor, his tears burning his face while guilt ate away at his soul.

Silence finally descended in the house, starting with the front door slamming shut as their father strode out of the house. As he pulled his hands away from his face, Declan felt the pull of dried blood from where his nose had bled, gluing his flesh together with a bloody seal.

As he got to his feet, his legs jelly beneath him, Declan feared the worst. He left his room and made his way to the stairs. Part of him expected to see his mother still standing there, daring him to come down, but she was gone.

It felt as if he were dreaming, his body, his actions and his thoughts, none of them in line, none of them really his, as Declan descended the stairs and moved into the living room.

He saw his brother on the floor, curled into a ball, weeping.

"Justin." He moved swiftly to cradle his brother. He didn't notice his mother standing to one side, watching her youngest suffer.

Justin flinched at the sound of his brother's voice, raising his head to show the black eye and bloody nose that he had gotten, all for nothing

"I'm so sorry, J," Declan sobbed, dropping to his knees beside his brother. "I'm so sorry,"

"Get away from him." Peggy's voice made Declan jump, sending him to his ass on the floor.

"Mum ... I ... why?" A thousand thoughts and questions buzzed through Declan's brain. When confronted with his father's rage, he crumbled; against his mother, he could force the words to the surface. Not with the same strength of voice as when he practiced in the car mirror, but he could give them a voice.

"He needs to learn his lesson. He is a liar and a filthy accident. He cursed our lives from the day he was born, and you will leave him there to learn or so help me God, Declan, I will call your father back for you." There was a something different in his mother's voice, a dullness to her eyes that told Declan that things were changing, and not in a good way.

Ignoring his mother, somehow finding a hidden strength in the face of a clear switch in patterns, he helped Justin to his feet, supporting almost all his brother's weight.

"I knew this would happen. You are spending too much time with him. Well, if you think you can carry on behaving like that bastard child, then go ahead, see what it gets you." Peggy's eyes seemed to turn an even deeper shade of black as she barked her threats, her body trembling as adrenaline surged through her bloodstream.

"He's my brother. It's me and him, all the way," Declan said, staring down his mother, while his insides felt as if they were about to melt through his trousers.

Peggy took a step forward, pulled back her hand, and slapped Declan across the face. He saw the blow coming but didn't move out of the way. He stood and took it, feeling happy that for once, it was not his brother.

The blow stung Declan's cheek, sending a burning spread of pain across his face until it felt as if half his head had been consumed by fire. Still, he gave no reaction, showed no sign of even noticing the slap. Turning his back on his mother, he helped his brother up the stairs.

"Don't worry, bro. We are getting out of here. School is over in a few weeks, and I'll find a job, then we can move out and get a place together. Leave this place behind." Declan placed his brother on his bed and sat down behind him at Justin's desk. He was not prepared to leave him alone.

Declan browsed through the artwork on the desk and found the image that his brother had been working on a few weeks before. The burning tenement block, the street littered with emergency services. With the color added to it, it almost looked real. Pulling it fully out of the stack of drawings, Declan took in every detail.

"You really have a gift, man." He replaced the image and scanned through some more, while Justin fell into an uneasy sleep.

CHAPTER FOUR

Justin took a week off work after the incident with his father. His eye was swollen and flared with all manner of angry colors. Justin kept predominantly to himself, not leaving his room unless it was to eat. Dinners had come to a silent, awkward affair. He ate quickly, despite his lack of appetite. The food was tasteless and bland; everything was the same.

With his plate clean, Justin would retreat upstairs once more and wait there until he was next forced to join his family.

Declan was not around much, as he was picking up extra shifts at the factory, desperate to both avoid the house and ensure his financial independence.

It was midway through the second week when Justin returned to work, his face causing much concern for Mr. Bukowski, who wanted to make sure Justin was up to the task of minding the store.

Justin was never sure if his boss understood that his store was not some thriving people magnet, but rather a slowly dying local convenience that most people ignored.

It was another particularly quiet night, and Justin was considering closing early. The shelves were stocked and everything that could be tidied away had been. There hadn't been a customer for almost twenty minutes and with only half an hour to go until closing time, Mr. Bukowski would not have minded. However, Justin didn't know where else he was going to go, and while closing early would solve one dilemma, it would be replaced with a worse one.

He was drifting away with his thoughts when he heard the door open and the chime of the bell rang through the store. It startled him, and when he looked up, he felt even more on edge. Cassie Martin was standing in the store, alone, and she was smiling at him.

"Sorry if I made you jump," she said with a grin. She moved towards the counter, and all Justin could think of was that she had nothing for him to ring up. "Oh my God, what happened to your face?"

A rush of heat flooded through him as the embarrassment of his home life came to the surface.

"Oh, nothing, I fell off my bike," Justin said, wondering if the words sounded more convincing to her than they did to him.

"Sure," she said, nodding, although it was clear from her expression that she didn't believe him.

"So, what are you going to do once you are closed up here?" she asked, leaning forward against the counter.

It was still early summer, but the weather had gotten warm and she was wearing a pair of jeans and a white cotton shirt that was loose enough to give Justin a perfect view when she leaned towards him.

"I'm not sure, I haven't thought about it yet," he said, trying to hide the shake in his voice.

He held Cassie's eye contact and felt as if he was sweating like a farmer in the heat of summer. Her eyes were a gentle shade of green, and her nose was peppered with freckles that made her look even more stunning. Her long auburn hair was loose, held in place by a simple headband.

"Well, if you don't have any plans, how about we take a drive?" She looked out of the window and pointed at the Ford parked in the lot in front of the store. "That is yours, right?"

"Yeah, well, my brother and I share it, but I've got the keys tonight." Justin smiled, worried he didn't sound too much like a dork. He felt relieved then Cassie laughed.

"Well, how about you and I take a little drive later on?" She leaned closer to the counter and smiled once more.

"I'd like that," Justin said, nodding, feeling the rest of the world melt away.

"Great," she said, hurrying around the counter to join him there. "I'll keep you company until you are ready."

At five foot six, Cassie was a few inches shorter than Justin, who had had a late growth spurt, and under all normal circumstances, she would be out of his league. While she was not part of the bitch-laden ruling clique of the school, she was popular, smart, and attractive. Justin didn't know what she saw in him, and in that moment, he didn't care. He just knew that he wasn't going to let it pass.

There was no sign of any customers, so Justin flipped the sign ten minutes early and shut up shop, after ringing up a bottle of vodka for Cassie. With the shop locked up for the night, Justin escorted Cassie out to his car. Sliding in beside her, Justin smiled, his nerves seemingly left behind in the story because he felt calm and on top of the world when he looked at her.

They drove away from the store and headed out of town. There was no motorway linked to the town, but they followed the main road, which ran all the way through Horn Hill. The lights of passing cars on the motorway grew bolder and bolder before them, and they had yet to really decide where they were going to go.

"Why don't we pull up over there somewhere? It's a beautiful night. We can have a drink and talk a little." Cassie smiled, and her eyes seemed to gleam in the night.

Justin swallowed hard, his heart thumping harder in his chest and echoing so loud in his ears he thought there could be no way that Cassie didn't hear it.

Justin turned off onto a small slip road that took them through the country on a winding road, surrounded by farmland.

Cassie leaned closer, and the flowery scent of her perfume filled the car, and Justin wondered how he had not smelled it before. It was possibly the greatest aroma he had ever encountered. Driving suddenly became a much more complicated affair, and when Cassie reached over and blew gently into his ear, Justin almost sent them off the road.

"This looks like a good spot," Cassie said, already climbing on Justin's lap.

She pulled out the bottle of vodka, as Justin fumbled with the key, shutting down the engine.

Cassie unscrewed the cap and drank from the bottle. She giggled, and took another drink, before offering the bottle to Justin. He moved to take it, but Cassie pulled it away, the smile on her face one that screamed mischief and made Justin's heart race even more.

Cassie giggled, and took a long drink from the vodka bottle before she lowered her mouth and kissed Justin, allowing the vodka to pass from one to the other.

The liquid burned as it went down, but Justin didn't care. He was hungry for more, and if that meant drinking vodka, then so be it.

The buzz of drink took control, and with it, their passion swiftly grew. Clothes were shed, and the troubles of the real world were shed too. Justin gave in to the overriding sensation of teenage lust he had never felt better. The only thing that Justin would have changed was the time it took for everything to end. He would have happily gotten lost in their embrace forever, not because he was foolish to think their tryst was necessarily true love conquering all, but because he was carefree and would have given anything in the world to remain so.

"Isn't it a beautiful night," Cassie said as the two of them sat on the hood of the car, staring up at the night sky.

"It sure is," Justin replied, letting out a slow, contented breath.

"You not a talker, are you?" Cassie asked, rolling onto her side to look at Justin.

"Me? I've never really thought about it," Justin said, turning to look at her. "I've never really had many people to chat with, only Declan."

"That's your brother, right? Are you two close?" Cassie pushed herself into a half-seated position, resting with her elbow on the windshield.

"I guess we are. I mean, we have each other's back." Justin wasn't sure how to answer, because every possibility brought his mind back to home, and what would undoubtedly be waiting for him.

"That's cool. I'm an only child. I guess that's why I'm always so chatty and stuff. You're different though. I like that." Cassie started giggling as she took another drink from the half-empty bottle of vodka. "You sure you don't want some more?"

"I'm good, I need to drive," Justin said, watching as Cassie took another drink.

"Good, then you can drive me home because I'm way too drive to be drunking." Cassie burst into another fit of giggles. Arching her back, she stared at Justin, licking her lips and blowing him a kiss before she stretched too far and fell from the hood of the car.

"Oh shit, are you alright?" Justin was on the ground and running to Cassie's aid, but he found her laughing to herself in the grass.

"I think I fell." Justin helped Cassie to her feet, holding her steady while she fought to find her balance.

"I think we should be getting you home now," he said to her, as he opened the passenger door and helped her into the passenger seat.

There wasn't room to turn around on the narrow path they had driven down, and after wrestling Cassie into both her seat and safety belt, Justin reversed the car back to the country road. This occurred much to Cassie's amazement. The drink was sinking into her cells now, and her state of inebriation continued to worsen until it reached the point, when Justin spun the car around and onto the main road, where she made him stop so she could lean out of the door and vomit.

"Are you alright?" Justin asked as he brushed Cassie's hair behind her ear and offered her a tissue to help dry her face.

She looked at him, her eyes unfocused, her face plastered with guilt.

"I'm sorry," she said, her lower lip quivering, foreshadowing the tears that were about to come.

"Hey, it happens. I've had to pick Declan up off the floor a few times." Justin thought back to a few months previous when Declan had passed out on the stairs, vomit covering his shirt and trousers. He had managed to get him upstairs and into bed without waking their parents, an act he considered to be a small miracle.

"No, I shouldn't have … it's just … life fucking sucks." Tears were flowing, and wet-sounding hiccups punctuated every few words that Cassie managed to utter.

"Yeah, tell me about it," Justin said, turning his attention back to the road.

"You wouldn't even know what it's like," Cassie scoffed. "To be afraid of coming home. Terrified of what will happen the minute someone says something he doesn't like."

The words cut Justin to the bone. Turning, he stared at Cassie, wondering if she were teasing him, if this whole thing was just some set up to prank the lonely kid from school. He saw her tears and heard her sharp breaths, and that thought fell away to nothing. Cassie closed her eyes as she tried to stop the tears, the pressure building in her face until she couldn't take it anymore.

"Your father … he … he hits you?" Justin asked, shocked. For so long, he never even thought about abuse happening to anybody else.

"He's my step-father. He doesn't hit me, but my mum. He drinks all the time and does whatever he wants to her. They think I'm asleep, but I hear it all. The things he said, the things he does." Cassie turned to look at Justin, exhaustion plastered over her face. "I'm sorry, I don't tell anybody this. I just wanted to have a fun night with a cute guy, and now look at me."

The lingering aroma of alcohol and vomit hung in the car, but Justin wouldn't have changed it. In that moment, he was exactly where he wanted to be. His heart started to race, and his hands were slick on the wheel. He swallowed hard, but his throat was suddenly as dry as Cassie's would be when she woke up in the morning.

"I understand," he said, his heart thundering in his chest, pumping so fast he couldn't breathe. His head started to spin, and that pre-faint warmth began to spread through him. "My face … it wasn't a fall from my bike. It was … it was … my father."

The world stopped. Justin's heart froze and everything ceased to matter. There was a moment when the words hung there, spoken but not yet processed by the one doing the listening, and it was both terrifying and exhilarating.

The words registered in Cassie's mind, and she turned to look at Justin, her features soft and caring. "What?"

"My dad, and my mum. They hate me. It doesn't matter what, everything comes back to me." Justin returned his attention to the road, unaware that he was crying, his whole body trembling as if he had caught a serious chill.

"And your brother?" Cassie asked, sounding soberer than she had been before the revelation.

"Declan tries to watch out for me. They never touch him. He can do no wrong, they just blame me." Justin loosened his grip on the wheel.

"I never knew. There was a reason I found you." Cassie reached out and her hand came to rest on Justin's, sitting on the gearstick.

Their eyes locked, and in that moment, their bond was sealed. Both smiled, and as Cassie closed her eyes and leaned back into the seat, she whispered, "Don't take me home. Take me away."

Justin was going to answer, but something moved out of the corner of his eye. Whipping his head around, he saw the fox dart out into the middle of the road. His reaction was instant and instinctive. He hit the brakes, turned the wheel, and called to Cassie to hold on.

Her eyes sprang open and a scream jumped from her mouth as she saw the trees along the verge coming towards her. Justin wrestled with the car, and the fox turned tail and charged back the way it had come.

The stop was a sudden one, and the crunch of metal and the high-pitched tone of breaking plastic rang out loud inside the car. The car stopped, its front passenger corner pressed against the trunk of a twisting oak tree.

"Are you okay?" Justin turned to look at Cassie, who was sitting with her eyes wide open, her chest rising and falling as if she had just finished running a race. "I am so sorry, the fox, it just came out of nowhere."

Justin started to babble, the words coming quicker and quicker, only being silenced when Cassie's lips found his. They were sour-tasting from the vomit, but it pulled Justin back into the present.

"It's okay. I'm fine." She smiled at him, and they fell into an embrace.

The car was not badly damaged, but the passenger light would need replacing. Driving carefully the rest of the way, Justin brought Cassie home and wrestled with letting her out of the car.

"I don't want you to get into trouble," he said as the car sat idling by the curb a few doors down from her house.

"I'll be fine. Dad will be passed out drunk by now, and like I said, he never touches me. I think if he did, my mum would kill him. It's you I'm worried about. Stay here, with me, or let's disappear together."

There was an urgency in her words, a seriousness that ran beneath the flight of fancy.

"I can't. I need to go back. I'll be alright. Let's meet tomorrow; we can spend the day together," Justin offered, already thinking up ways they could spend the day, to keep them both safe and away from trouble.

"It's Sunday, I have to go to church in the morning, but pick me up at noon, and I'm all yours." Cassie leaned over and gave Justin another kiss, staring into his eyes.

Getting out of the car, she was a little unsteady on her feet but managed to make it to her front door. Justin sat watching, waiting for her to disappear inside before he swung the car around and went home.

He parked the car with the broken headlight pressed against the wall, hoping he could get some rest, and get up to find a place to fix it before it was seen. His parents never used their car, as they both had one of their own. Justin saw no reason they would have to notice, and he would tell Declan in the morning.

The house was silent, as he followed his carefully planned rout up to his room. He collapsed into bed a little after two in the morning and was asleep in seconds.

The first thing he knew about the dawning of the new day was when Declan started shaking him in his bed.

"Justin, you need to wake up, something's happened." The fear in Declan's voice had him awake in seconds, the need for more sleep pushed from his mind, as the adrenaline started flowing.

"What's going on?" Justin asked, memories of the previous night still flirting with his brain.

"I don't know, but Dad's really kicking off. I don't like it; I've never heard him like this." Declan's face was pale and his eyes were wide.

It was only then that the bellow of his father echoed up the stairs and finally reached Justin's ears. He went stiff in his bed, as his blood froze in his veins.

"Shit, he knows." Justin snatched at the words as the cold realization dawned on him.

"He knows what? Justin, what happened?" Declan asked, his words as serious as a house fire.

"Last night, I ... I crashed the car." The words felt heavy to say and sank the moment he spoke them. "Not bad, just broke the light trying to miss a fox. I was going to get it fixed today, once I picked Cassie up. I didn't think Dad would notice."

"Cassie?" Declan asked, raising an eyebrow.

"Not the time, bro," Justin corrected him, fear and adrenaline coursing through his veins. "I need to get out of here."

Justin leaped from the bed and scrambled around the room, getting dressed as he found each item.

The door to the room flew open just as Justin was slipping his last shoe onto his foot. The door flew into the wall behind it with such force that the handle became embedded in the drywall.

"You useless cunt," Jackson roared, his face a deep maroon and sheened with rage-driven sweat.

He lunged at Justin who evaded his first grab but had nowhere left to turn to miss the second. Jackson grabbed his youngest son by the hair and yanked him over the bed towards the hallway.

"Dad, I can explain," Justin shrieked, terrified.

"Shut your mouth! You think you can crash a car and hide it from me. What did you do, you little shit? Hey, tell me!" Jackson's hands found his son's throat and started choking him, squeezing not with an abusive anger, but with murderous rage. His eyes bulged, while thick white spittle foamed in the corners of his mouth.

Peggy came up the stairs and saw the way her husband had snapped, and for the first time in her life tried to pull him away from Justin.

"That's enough," she screamed, yanking on her husband's arm, but a backhand across the cheek shut her up and put her on her ass on the floor.

Declan was there too, and while Justin fought to stay alive, his vision was fading as his body screamed out for oxygen. His hands clenched down on his father's but barely made a dent in the muscular forearms. Justin kicked out in desperation, but a knee to his gut stopped him, driving the remaining air from his lungs, accelerating the rate at which he passed out.

Then suddenly, the pressure was gone. The darkness came and went, like a light with a faulty dimmer switch. Justin's heart thumped slow and steady in his ears, speeding up as he started to gulp down deep breaths, his throat burning with a white-hot agony.

His father stood before him, his eyes wide, but in surprise rather than rage. Blood replaced the spittle in his mouth, and he dropped to his knees on the floor.

Justin looked at his father and up to Declan. His brother was standing there with a bloody pair of scissors in his hands, his eyes wide and focused only on their father.

"Leave him alone!" Declan roared as he stabbed again, and again, driving the scissors repeatedly into his father's back, sending a shower of blood spatter over the hallway, adding to it each time he withdrew the knife and swung it back down to find flesh once more.

Declan roared, Peggy screamed, and Justin collapsed, unable to support himself anymore. The carpet was soaked with blood, and Declan stood, drenched in the thick, red substance. He was panting and the scissor blades were bent and twisted in his hands. Their father lay on the floor, his body barely recognizable as human, the flesh cleaved open, exposing bone and bubbled sections of minced flesh. The metallic scent of blood was thick in the air. Justin looked at his brother, while Peggy collapsed to the floor, stroking her husband's head, talking to him, apologizing to him over and over again.

When she finally raised her head, her eyes fell on Justin and her hatred boiled over. "I hate you. I always regretted the day you were shat into this world. Get out of my house." The words, although spoken through tears, did not need to be repeated. Justin rose to his feet, aware that he too was covered in blood, and walked out into the garden where he sat down on the small porch. His body was trembling as his brain tried to process everything that had happened. He looked over at the car, tucked neatly away where he had left it. There was no way his father could have accidentally seen the damage.

A shadow loomed over him. Justin looked up as Declan sat down beside him, looking like the final survivor in a *Halloween* movie.

"Mum's called the police." Declan spoke the words with a strange calm in his voice, almost as if it were the most natural sentence in the world.

"Now what?" Justin asked, looking at his brother, not even seeing the cover of gore.

"Now you're safe," Declan said, putting his tacky arm around Justin's shoulders.

"Why did you do that? You're going to go to jail." Justin held back the tears as the emotions started hitting him.

"That's just what big brothers do," he whispered, as the neighborhood started to scream.

CHAPTER FIVE

It was the talk of the town, gossip that fueled the mouths of housewives and anybody else that cared to join for weeks. A boy murdering his own father. The eulogy published in the paper painted a hideous lie, which Justin was confronted with daily.

Jackson Howland, a loving husband, and a doting father cut down in the prime of his life by a troubled boy. Justin's mother had a field day playing the role of grieving victim, forgetting both Justin and Declan, living a double life. The grieving public face and the evil parent behind closed doors. Justin had often wondered if his parents really were the ones to blame. Perhaps they had a condition that predisposed them to behave in such a way. Now, in the wake of his father's death, Justin came to learn exactly how cold-blooded and evil his mother really was.

She never looked at Justin, not outside, and not inside. He was treated like a ghost in his own home. Declan was similarly shunned. He was wiped from their lives; childhood photos were ripped from the walls and thrown into boxes, left by the trash. His mother never visited Declan and the tale she told the police was a complete fabrication. Justin's own statement was discredited by her continued insistence that he would say anything to keep Declan out of trouble.

It was those lies that had led to his current predicament, stuck in a police interview room, sitting opposite a large police officer with a thick goatee and an even thicker gut. His face was blotchy and sweat gave him a permanent sheen, almost as if his face had been varnished to give it a real finish. The stench of cigarettes wafted from him, blown Justin's way every time the officer moved or spoke.

"I already told you everything," Justin said, irritated at having been asked the same question for the sixth time. He also needed to pee, a fact that was getting harder and harder to ignore.

"Yes, you said your father has abused you for years. Your mother too. You claim that your father was trying to kill you when Declan intervened, defending you." The cop read from his notes, but Justin knew it was all an act.

"Yes," he answered, knowing that they would not take his word for it.

"Then tell me, why did you not mention this before? Why did you and your brother stay in the house where you were abused?" The cop sat back and crossed his arms over his chest. His large forearms bulged with muscles the rest of body lacked.

"Because I was afraid. You don't understand, this has been going on since I was a kid. I don't remember a time when I wasn't afraid, and Declan, well, Declan was different. They loved him. Everything was my fault." Justin felt the cracks appearing, and before he could do anything to stop it, they burst open into tears.

Grief consumed him, ripping open the cracks, turning them into deep fissures carved all the way down to Justin's soul, where the anger and the grief he had stored up for so long could finally well up and burst free.

The tears were hot and scalding at first, but after a few moments, the pressure dropped, and Justin felt their soothing presence. He stared at the cop, who sat unmoved and unfazed by the display he was seeing.

"Are you done?" he asked, when Justin sat panting, his head resting on the cool surface of the table.

"Yes," Justin managed to exhale.

"Good, then I have to ask you, even if your brother was acting in self-defense, why did he carry on? Why did he keep attacking your father long after he had stopped attacking you?" Something in the officer's face had changed. His eyes were watching Justin with interest now.

"Because he had had enough of it. Eighteen years is a long time to live in an abusive home. This was the final straw." Justin raised his head and stared at the officer, his vision blurred through tears.

"Thank you, Mr. Howland, you are free to leave. If you wish to make any formal complaints of abuse, then feel free, but as of now, this discussion is over." The officer stood and adjusted the tight waistband of his trousers, then took a crumbled-up paper napkin out of his pocket, and wiped the sweat from his forehead with it, before tossing it into the bin in the corner of the room.

"What about Declan?" Justin asked, half expecting the officer to have seen the light and set his brother free also.

"Your brother is under arrest for murder. He is not going anywhere, but I am sure, when this thing goes to court, the abuse angle will be used. My advice, get your story straight. I'm not saying you're lying, I'm just saying, make sure your head is on straight because they will play this against you as much as your team will play it to help." The officer opened the door and let Justin leave, following him down the corridor to the lift and escorting him to the main reception area.

Three people sat waiting in the room, but Justin paid them no mind, not until someone called his name.

"Justin, Justin, wait up." The voice followed him outside, where he stood with his hands in his pockets, wondering what he was going to do next.

He turned when he finally recognized his name being called and was almost bowled over by the charging figure of Cassie. She flung herself at him, her arms wrapping around him, locking him in her embrace. Her perfume filled his nose and his head swam; the shouts and the screams inside his head died down in an instant. He had found his peace with her.

"Oh my God, I'm so sorry. I've been trying to get hold of you, but your mother, well, she wouldn't let me in." Cassie's eyes were stung with tears.

"I'm so sorry about all this. I can't believe all of this. How is Declan?" she asked, firing questions at a rapid pace.

"I don't know. I've not seen him yet. I was brought here to talk about … well, you know, everything that happened to me." Justin took a deep breath and found himself clearer headed than he had been in the days since his father's death.

"Well, don't worry. You can come with us, can't he, Grandpa?" Cassie turned to the older man that had followed her out of the station.

"Well, we should probably be introduced to each other first." The old man smiled. His face was wrinkled by time, but his eyes shone with a vitality that said he had a lot more gas left in the tank.

"Oh … of course, Justin, this is my grandpa, Everett. I am living with him now. After everything that happened to you, I … I couldn't live in silence anymore." Cassie's lip started quivering, and she buried her face into Justin's neck.

"I'm sorry," he whispered, holding her.

"Cassie here told me a little about your situation, and well, if you want, there is always space at our table. We've got a big enough place, and it's close enough to get to school and back. Especially for those last few weeks before the summer." There was an honest kindness to the words, and it almost brought Justin to his knees. His head was spinning with everything that had happened, but he never doubted the offer for a second.

"I would be thrilled if I could stay," he said, looking from Everett down to Cassie, whose face was almost split in two by the smile that had spread across her face.

"Then that settles it. I'll show you the way home, and you can get settled in," Everett said, turning and heading back to his car which had been parked, Justin was sure, under no accidental conditions, right next to his own.

"I'll ride with Justin, just to make sure he finds the way," Cassie called, her hand sliding into his, their fingers interlocking.

"Okay, honey," Everett said as he walked away.

"What's happening?" Justin asked as he was half dragged by Cassie over to the car.

"I'll explain everything as we drive, but trust me, everything is going to be alright now." She looked up and gave Justin a kiss on the cheek. Her lips felt like a cooling balm and sent a welcome chill running through him.

They drove for a while in silence, the radio offering a gentle background noise that neither of them was really listening to. After pulling out of the police station, they turned right, heading in the opposite direction to Justin's house. The realization hit him like a slap in the face, and his breath suddenly started to increase.

"Hey, hey, it's going to be okay," Cassie said, her hand coming to rest on top of his on the steering wheel.

"It's all happening kind of fast. I'm so confused," Justin spoke, unsure what he was going to say until the words came out, his brain somehow managing to make some sense out of the thousands of thoughts and feelings that were swirling around inside his head, like some inner-cranial hurricane.

"I know, and listen, I'm only doing this to help you. If you want to leave or go do your own thing, then you can. I just wanted to do something," Cassie said, her green eyes focused on him, and he felt the spark between them. It was more than just two people trying to escape a bad part of their lives.

"I wouldn't leave you for the world," Justin said, the words feeling like the most natural ones he had ever spoken.

Cassie smiled, her nose wrinkling just a little, making her look even cuter. "You need to take a right up here."

Cassie's maternal grandparents lived on a large property outside of town, an old farmhouse that had been in the family for some generations. Cassie's mother grew up with six brothers and two sisters, and the house had easily accommodated them all. It was a warm house from the outside, the driveway leading up to it lined by apple trees, and the three large fields that lay on both sides and to the rear were maintained but not used for any farming purposes. Although, Justin did see a decent-sized vegetable garden off to one side of the house.

"This place is huge," he said as they sat in the car, staring up at the house. Justin needed a few moments to gather his thoughts.

"Come on, we can do this." Cassie gave his leg a reassuring squeeze, and together they got out of the car.

Everett was already in the house, and as they walked up, the door opened and Cassie's grandmother appeared. While Justin had never met Cassie mother, it was clear from which side of the family she got her looks. Her grandmother, a woman in her sixties, or so Justin would guess, had the same shade of green eye color, and the same gentle, delicate nose.

"You must be Justin, you poor thing." The old woman pulled Justin into a strong embrace and held him for a long time. "Anything you need, you just tell us. You are welcome to stay here as long as you need."

"Justin, this is my grandmother, Rose," Cassie said, introducing the pair, standing with her arm locked around Justin's.

"Come on inside, I've got some soup cooking and the bread was finished this morning, so it still has a bit of warmth to it. You must be famished." Rose turned and disappeared back inside the house.

"Are you alright?" Cassie asked, looking up at Justin.

"Me? Yes, I'm good. This is just a lot to take in. I mean, where are your parents?" Justin asked, stepping over the threshold the moment the aroma of homemade soup hit him.

"After everything that happened with you, I just, I had to tell someone about things. My grandpa has always been my best friend, and when I told him, he just held me and let me cry. They took me in without question, and my mother, well, she won't leave. It worries them sick, knowing what he is like, but they can't force her to leave." Cassie brought her voice down to a whisper as they got closer to the kitchen.

The kitchen was a large farmhouse affair, with lots of natural wood and windows, allowing for the light to pass over the garden and into the kitchen. Rose stood by the stove, ladling soup into two large bowls, while a plate stacked high with thick slices of fresh bread stood on the table.

Justin and Cassie sat down, opposite each other at the table, their gazes locked. They ate in silence, and both Everett and Rose gave them space.

"It's good, right?" Cassie said, slurping slightly at the soup.

"It's incredible," Justin answered, coating a piece of bread with soft butter and dipping it into the bowl.

When their lunch was finished, Justin felt better than he had in a long time. He was worried about Declan but had faith that things were starting to turn around.

"Here, let me show you around," Cassie said, getting up from the table. She took Justin's hand and led him through the house, telling stories of how she had spent a lot of time there when she was young. She spoke with ease and had a storyteller's voice. Justin gladly listened and wanted to hear more.

"My bedroom is down the end here, and you can take anyone you want. Personally, I'd recommend that one." She pointed to the room next to hers. "It's got a great view, and is right next to mine."

"Then I'm sold," Justin answered, as the urge to pull Cassie into his arms consumed him. "Are you sure it's alright for me to stay here?" Justin asked, feeling compelled to clarify this was not a dream or some final twisted idea designed to break him by showing him a slice of happiness and rip it away from him.

"Of course, you are more than welcome. Here, let me show you out back." Cassie's enthusiasm was growing by the minute, and she all but ran out of the house, dragging Justin behind her.

The rear of the house was a bare dirt area, flattened through generations of use, from horse and cart through working farm equipment, and now as a parking area for three different vehicles, including an old van that looked as if it had been abandoned there. From there, the yard bled neatly into a long open field, with a line of trees running down the right and across the rear, natural boundary markers, laid back in a time before contracts and lawyers were needed to come to an agreement. The grass was more overgrown in the rear than the more publicly visible areas.

"Come on, there is a great spot just down here," Cassie said, still dragging Justin by the hand.

They disappeared into the knee-deep grass and were soon swallowed from view as the field rolled down a slope which had been invisible to the eye from up at the house.

They drew closer to the tree line but were stopped by a small creek that ran along the edge of the field. It was a picturesque setting, the sun behind the trees, starting its descent, the shadow growing slowly longer. The shade still held the warmth of the day, and as they sat on a fallen tree, the world became a peaceful have around them.

They pair inched closer, the physical attraction between them growing now, and with no need for containment. Cassie played with her hair, sweeping it over her far shoulder, while she twisted her body on the log. Justin moved closer, leaning forward when he felt something brush against the back of his hand. He thought it was Cassie, reaching for him, her fingers tracing a gentle pattern on his skin. But then she raised her hand to her face and the tickling sensation continued. Looking down, Justin saw the two beetles chasing over his skin.

His blood froze as he watched their hardened back bodies scurry over his flesh, his senses heightened to the point where he felt the prick of each leg against his skin. He began to sweat and shake, his eyes fixated on the bugs. His hands began to shake, while he fought back the urge to scream.

"Justin, Justin, what's wrong?" Cassie asked, seeing the change in his attitude. She reached out to him, shaking him by the shoulder as if trying to take him from his trance. "Oh my God, you're sweating."

When Justin couldn't put together an answer, Cassie looked for herself, following his line of vision down to his hand where both beetles had reached his wrist.

Casually, as if it were nothing, Cassie reached out and swatted them away. Justin watched as their bodies tumbled through the air. Only when they landed in the grass and he accepted that they were gone did his wits return to him.

"I'm ... I'm sorry," he stammered. "I don't like bugs. They remind me of when my mother used to lock me up in the shed."

Justin shivered as he spoke about the memory and hated himself for appearing so weak. "Sorry I ruined this. It's beautiful here."

"You didn't ruin anything." Leaning in, Cassie kissed him on the lips and held his lips against hers for a time thereafter. "There you go."

Her eyes twinkled with mischief when she smiled, and Justin hoped that he would be able to drown in it.

They fell silent for a while, sitting in the peace, happy to let the world build up around them again.

"How did you learn to cope?" Cassie asked, her voice almost bashful.

"Declan," Justin said with almost without hesitation. "He was always there for me. He would pull me out of the shed and brush the insects off me. He would clean my face and get cold cloths for the bruises and the swellings."

Justin shuddered as he thought of the bugs, and he could feel them crawling all over him, their tiny legs multiplying until it felt as if his skin was on fire. He knew it was illogical, just a stupid trick of his mind, but he couldn't stop it. The urge to swat at himself, to scratch himself until his skin was raw consumed him.

Cassie sat staring at him. "It's okay," she spoke softly. "There's nothing on you."

"What about you? What happened to your parents?" Justin asked, wanting to change the subject, to take his mind away from the bugs, which he kept telling himself were not clawing their way back to him, like some unconquered quest they needed to fulfill. His flesh could not be that sweet.

"Well, this is going to sound a bit corny, but after I heard about what happened, I just knew that I couldn't leave it any longer. I had to do something, and so I told my grandparents everything. They moved me in without question and tried to convince my mum to leave, but she wouldn't. She keeps claiming there was nothing going on. That I was mistaken or making it up for some reason." Cassie lowered her gaze, as if she intended to study the ground where her feet were placed.

"So, she's still with him?" Justin couldn't understand that. He had been abused his whole life and couldn't wait until he was able to leave his parents behind.

"Yep, and I always thought she was just staying with him because of me. Turns out, she actually loves the son of a bitch. Kind of twisted, right?" Cassie forced a laugh, but Justin could both see and hear the pain that lurked just beneath the surface.

"How do you cope?" Justin asked, curious.

"I drink." The laugh, however fake it was, fell away, and a deadly seriousness filled the space it left. "I know I shouldn't, but sometimes … most of the time, it just takes it all away. It makes me numb, and I like that." Cassie shifted on the log, wrapping her arms around herself.

Justin wanted nothing more than to pull her close to him, but he couldn't. He was fighting too many of his own problems at that moment, and it held him back.

"We should be getting back to the house," Cassie said after a time. "It's going to be getting chilly soon, once the sun disappears behind the trees, and we have some chores to do before dinner." She stood and turned to Justin, waiting for him to stand too. "I'm really happy you are here."

Their dinner that evening was a hearty home-cooked feast, unlike anything Justin had seen before. It was a simple affair in terms of content. Beef so tender that it fell apart just by looking at it, creamy potatoes and vibrant-colored vegetables, topped off with a thick, rich gravy, but to Justin, it tasted like a slice of heaven.

He and Cassie sat together, side-by-side, and for most of the meal, their right and left hand respectively were locked.

"This is delicious, Mrs. ..." Justin froze, unsure what Cassie's maternal grandparents' surname was.

"You call me Rose, young man, and you are more than welcome." Rose was a kind-hearted woman. That was clear to see. She shone at the table, looking around at the family that she had been given.

After they were finished eating, Justin and Cassie did the dishes, one washing, one drying, like a well-oiled machine.

The day had been a long one and had taken its toll on Justin. He excused himself at nine o'clock that evening and headed up to his room. When he was alone, the peace didn't last long, but the stresses that came to him were still somewhat dulled by the knowledge that he had escaped. He felt guilty at having not thought about Declan too much. It hurt to think of his brother sitting cold and lonely in some prison cell. He chided himself for not having found a way to get him out of prison. The concept that his brother might end up in jail still hadn't truly dawned on him. It was a fact that he was tactically ignoring.

Justin was tired, but no matter how hard he tried, sleep just would not come for him. He tossed and turned and watched the clock. The hours passed, and Justin heard Cassie head to bed also. Her footsteps in the hall made his heart flutter and brought him back down from the stupor he had been in.

A while later, there was a knock at his door. Unsure what to say, Justin sat up in bed and waited, wondering if maybe he had dreamed it.

There was no second knock, but the handle turned and the door opened. Cassie pushed her head inside and quickly stumbled through the door, tripping as she did. Giggling to herself, she closed the door and stood up on unsteady feet.

"Hey, you," she slurred, drunk again.

"Hey, are you okay?" Justin asked, half out of bed to go to her.

"Fuck yeah, I'm great," she slurred, charging across the room to pounce on Justin before he could stand.

From close by, the alcohol haze hung like a cloud.

"How much have you had to drink?" Justin asked, as he looked over at the clock. It hadn't been too long since she came up, so whatever her answer was, she had drunk it quickly.

"What does it matter?" Cassie asked, her lips finding Justin neck, eager to taste whatever piece of flesh she could find.

"It's not a healthy way ..." Justin paused as her head shot up, her eyes blazing.

"I'm fine. I've had a skinful, and now I want to fuck, are you in?" Cassie asked, her words straightforward and laced with fire.

Justin wanted to say no. He wanted to tell her to lie down with him and to let things drift away, but as she straddled him, her body moving to the same silent rhythm as his, he was whipped down a wild river of hormones and lust. Stopping suddenly became the last thing he wanted to do.

When it was all over, they lay in the bed, naked, their bodies tacky with sweat, and Cassie cried herself to sleep. Justin held her, enjoying the sensation of her body against his. He found a peace in her presence and drifted off to sleep more concerned about Cassie and the road she was heading down than he was about himself.

The days moved on apace, blurring into one another. With school ramping up and about to end, chores around the home, and the ongoing legal problems with his brother, Justin was happy to just make it to his bedroom in the evening. Declan was being tried for voluntary manslaughter, and his legal team had spent the afternoon briefing Justin on the changes of escaping a conviction and were trying to get Declan to plead guilty in exchange for a lighter sentence.

Declan looked like a broken figure sitting in the county jail. He was pale and dirty, his eyes tired and sunk deep into his face. Their mother had still not visited him, and Justin felt terrible that he was unable to do anything more to help his brother.

"If he doesn't change his plea, there's a chance they will push it up to second-degree murder. Then he is looking at twenty-five years." Justin heard the words, but he didn't really comprehend them. He understood what he was being told, but it just didn't really sink in that this was his brother they were talking about.

"It wasn't murder," Justin said, his body trembling inside his jacket.

"Son, your father is dead. He was stabbed twenty-seven times. That's murder. However, if Declan pleads guilty, they will charge him with voluntary manslaughter, and then he's looking at fifteen years, so he could even be out in less than ten, depending on how the trial goes, and how well he behaves once he is inside." The lawyer, whose name Justin had heard and forgotten just as quickly, sat with Justin in one of the private consultation rooms the county jail had to offer.

"What do you want me to do?" Justin asked.

"Talk to him. Get him to understand what is going on. He seems to be shutting down on us, and that's not a good thing for this case, and it won't be a good thing for him once he gets inside. That's the important thing to understand here. I know it's hard, but you need to face the fact that your brother is going to go to jail. The question is not about if, but about how long." The words had a sobering effect on Justin, like a bucket of ice water thrown over a dozing soul. He sat up straight in the chair, the words echoing inside his head.

"Declan can't go to prison." It wasn't a question, it was a statement, a simple fact which he would not allow to play out any differently.

"It's too late for that argument. What's done is done. We really are on damage control here. You need to speak to him." The lawyer stood and placed a hand on Justin's shoulder. "I am really sorry about this."

He walked out of the room, leaving Justin alone with his thoughts. He only snapped out of it when his brother appeared in front of him, helped into his chair by two prison guards. Both men studied Justin for a moment before leaving the room.

The two brothers stared at each other, neither saying a word. Their eyes both told the same story, and neither was truly ready to face the reality of their situation.

"That lawyer said they want to charge you with murder," Justin said, the words sounding alien to him.

"I know," Declan answered, his voice cold and emotionless.

"They want you to plead guilty," Justin added.

"I know."

"Declan," Justin began, but his brother raised his head, his sunken eyes were wet with tears.

"I get it, Jay, I really do. I killed the old man, and you know what, I'd do it again too. I just wish I had done it earlier." The words had a bite to them, a truth that resonated deeper than the emotions that were consuming them both.

"Don't say that," Justin said, looking around nervously, expecting guards to come storming in.

"It's the truth. You didn't deserve a life like that, and I'm sorry it took me so long to stand up for you." The remorse was genuine, and the pain and guilt built up through the years were finally being allowed to run free.

"Declan, I ..." Justin couldn't find the words.

"I'll plead guilty. Don't worry. Just promise me you will get out. Get away from this place." Declan pleaded with his brother. "Don't stay here for me. Get out and live your own life, brother."

"I ... I already left home. Mum won't talk to me. She plays this grieving widow role; she is telling everybody bad things about you."

Justin didn't know how much Declan knew, or how much he should be telling him, but he was the only real family he had left.

"That doesn't matter. She's just as broken as our old man was. I'm happy you are out." Declan smiled. "Where are you staying? I've got some savings. I'll give you my codes, you can take it all."

"I'm staying with a girl from school. Cassie Martin." Justin wasn't sure if Declan would remember her. It had been two years since he left.

"She was the cute blonde in your year, right?" Declan answered almost immediately.

"That's the one." Justin smiled.

"Well done, brother." Declan slapped the table and the pair laughed. It was uneasy, and forced, but for a moment everything felt as if it would be alright.

"She's had her problems too. Her dad beats her mother, but she escaped and now we both live with her grandparents." Justin found himself relaxing as if he and Declan were sitting in a pub, chatting about the week rather than sitting in a prison room.

"Poor girl. You look after her, Jay." Declan's voice got serious in an instant; there was something in his eyes that changed and altered the entire tone of his words.

"I will. She's got her own problems she needs to face." Justin thought about the drinking, which was becoming a nightly occurrence now. Cassie would stumble into his room, stinking of alcohol, some nights worse than others. They would fuck and she would cry herself to sleep while he held her.

Once he had tried to say no, to just hold her, but she insisted. She had gotten mad and screamed at him. That night, she wept as they fucked, and vomited in the toilet before passing out in bed. Justin remained by her side, holding her. In the morning, sober and with clear eyes, Cassie climbed onto him again, holding him until they had to get out of bed and prepare for the day.

"Take care of her; she sounds like she needs you. Get away from this place. Get away from me. I'm serious, Jay," Declan interrupted Justin before he had a chance to voice is disagreement. "I know you, and I know you would be here every week to visit. I don't want that. I want you to go and live your life, write me, visit now and then, but don't get lost just because I'm here."

Justin promised and hugged his brother, an act that was quickly broken up by the guards, who seemed angry at their parting embrace. The tears that traced down Justin's cheeks and over his lips as his brother was pulled away tasted bitter and made Justin's skin crawl.

He didn't say anything that afternoon, or during dinner, where he mostly played with his food.

That night, Cassie brought the alcohol with her, and they both drank to excess, as a way to silence the screams of reality.

CHAPTER SIX

August 27th, 2017

The scream that rang out of the bathroom cut through the house like a howling winter wind. It brought people running as if expecting to stop some gruesome murder from taking place.

"There, there, I saw it in the window." The girl stood in the middle of the bathroom, pointing at the large frosted-glass window.

"What did you see, honey?" Justin asked, crouching down to talk to his daughter.

"A spider, a huge one," Chelsea, his ten-year-old daughter cried, appearing to border on the edge of full hysteria.

"Well, let me take a look." Justin stood back up and grabbed a towel from the rack.

Moving across the bathroom, the warm tiles beneath his feet, he watched the window sill. It was filled with various products and cosmetics, a hazard that came from living in a house with four women.

"I don't see anything," he said before correcting himself. "Wait, I see him." Moving a bottle of shampoo, which happened to be the only thing on the ledge that was his, he saw the fat-bodied spider cowering in the corner.

He gently picked up the creature in a towel, opened the large part of the window, and dropped the arachnid onto the outer ledge.

"He was scared and probably just looking for a way out." Justin dropped the towel and turned to look at his daughter.

Chelsea stood with her arms crossed, a pout on her lips and one eyebrow raised in an accusing arc above her cool green eyes; her mother's eyes.

"You don't think I'm ever going to use that towel again, do you?" Chelsea's other eyebrow rose to join its counterpart.

"It's fine. I'll put it straight in the wash," Justin said, making a show of opening the hamper and throwing the towel inside.

"Ugh," Chelsea groaned, turning to leave the room. "You just don't get it."

She was right. After a wife and three daughters, Justin still didn't get it.

"What was that all about?" Cassie asked as Justin returned downstairs.

"Spider," Justin said, collapsing back down onto the sofa beside his wife.

"Well, that explains the scream," Cassie said as she took a drink of wine from the glass.

"Did I miss anything?" Justin asked, settling under the blanket beside his wife.

"Nope, just a lot of talking. Oh, one woman got her tits out, but she was dead, so I guess it kind of cancels it out a little." She took another drink and smiled at Justin.

"Yeah, I'd rather a breast not be cold," he replied. "Unless they were yours."

"Well, that got dark in a hurry," Cassie said after half-choking on a sip of wine.

"You know what I mean," Justin told her, repositioning his arm around her shoulders.

"Lucky for you, I do." Cassie leaned over and kissed Justin full on the lips.

"Is there a little leftover for me?" he asked, looking at the wine bottle on the small table beside the sofa.

"Um, no this one is empty, but there is another one in the kitchen." Cassie fluttered her eyes.

"Okay, I'll go grab it." Justin got up and walked through to the kitchen, grabbing the uncorked bottle of Merlot from the kitchen side.

He filled both glasses and settled back down to finish the movie.

As was often the case, Cassie fell asleep midway through, having had a busy day chasing after the kids and looking after the house, a task she insisted on taking care of herself, in spite of the fact that they had more than enough money to hire someone in.

Justin watched the movie, yet he found it difficult to concentrate on what he was watching. The movie was one he had seen before, but still, he found himself unable to follow the chain of events that built up to the fiery ending. As he went to refill his glass, Justin was shocked to find the bottle was already empty. He looked over at Cassie, her face just as cute now as it had been some twenty-five years earlier, he gave a sigh. It was the second night in a row she had drunk herself to sleep again. He understood why. It was the same reason why he was having trouble sleeping. It was that time of year. The anniversary of the worst, and yet, best things to ever happen to them both. It had been twenty-five years since Justin's father had died; a quarter of a century since Cassie had fled her abusive home, over half their lives ago that they came together in her grandparent's farmhouse.

Justin understood Cassie's need to drink. Anything that dulled the senses to the lingering memories which were always aching and raw, no matter how many years had passed. Although his demons only rose for a short time every year, Cassie battled hers daily. It was the time of year that Justin felt most distant to his wife. He was always forced to confront everything that had happened. He had met Cassie, and as a result, his father had died. It was a complicated fact that he had avoided thinking about for many years, but after many therapy sessions, he uncovered the hidden fact behind everything.

He bore no grudges and held Cassie accountable for nothing, but he had been forced to confront the fact that his father's death came because of an accident he had while driving Cassie home. Everything else that had happened to him was a direct result of that same moment.

He was thankful for it, a fact that he had struggled with. He knew he hated his father, but he had never wanted to admit he was truly glad that he was dead. His life had improved dramatically that day, with a single exception. He lost his best friend and brother.

On the sofa, Cassie gave a snort and rolled over, her empty wine glass falling from her hands onto the thick rug that covered the floor space between the two sofas. Justin stared at it for a while before reaching over to place it on the coffee table, where it stood beside the empty bottles.

Cassie drank, and that was something they had both learned to live with. She functioned fine, and only drank in the evenings, most days. Although, there were some when she just needed it more than others, and on those days, the evening was never enough.

As he sat back, considering just heading to bed, even though he knew he wouldn't sleep, Justin grabbed the letter he had received a few days earlier.

It was from the Hammerhead Penitentiary, where his brother was being held. His release had been finalized. In two days, Declan Howland would be a free man for the first time in twenty-five years.

The concept terrified Justin. Not because he didn't want his brother to be free, but because he was scared of how society would accept his him. Would Declan still have a chance to build a life, or would his father still have the final laugh from beyond the grave?

He had yet to tell Cassie the news, mainly because the question he would immediately follow it up with was if Declan could stay with them until he got back on his feet. He knew that Cassie would have no problem with it. She understood his past and the bond he had with his brother, but it was still something that would open up old wounds, for both of them.

Shutting off the television, Declan took Cassie into his arms and carried her up the stairs. Her body was as light and petite as ever, and despite having had three children, relatively close together, she worked hard to keep herself in shape.

Once in bed, Cassie's gentle snores punctuated the silence, as Justin lay with his wife in his arms, his eyes slowly closing, as the temptation of sleep grew too much for him to bear.

CHAPTER SEVEN

Declan sat in his cell, the bed next to him empty. His cellmate, a man by the name of Ricard, had been moved out two days prior, leaving Declan alone with his thoughts. With his release confirmed, each day had become the same slow nightmare that had been the first six months of his sentence.

It was his last morning, and all of his belongings were bundled up and ready to go, his feet tapping a nervous beat on the floor.

A knock at the door stole his attention away from the wait. It was Winston, an older man who had taken Declan under his wing when he first arrived. Serving two life sentences for a double homicide he committed back in the late sixties, Winston found spirituality and dedicated his life Buddhism. He was a large, peaceful man, with a muscular and tattoo-covered exterior. Declan would miss him greatly

"I just wanted to pop by and say thank you," Winston said, his voice soft and thoughtful. Each word was spoken with reason.

"Thank me?" Declan asked, never quite sure where their conversations would go. A life of incarceration had not stopped the old man from becoming wise, wiser he reasoned, than a great many people on the outside.

"Yes, thank you for letting me help you, and guide you. When you arrived, you were scared and angry, and I have seen that combination swallow people whole in here. But you kept your head down, and you did the right thing each time." Winston smiled, his large teeth impeccably white.

"Not every time," Declan said, looking down at the scars on his hands. He had been jumped in the cafeteria, almost a year after he had arrived. Two men started beating on him until something snapped inside of him. He wrapped a metal food tray around one man's head and punched the other so many times his knuckles bled.

"We all make mistakes, Declan, and while your path is not mine, and mine is not yours, there are times when you must defend yourself. In here, the rules are different. They are slight, but they are different nonetheless. You did what you needed to do, and I know that once you are outside, you will do what you need to do there too."

"Thank you." Declan stood up and walked to the open door of his cell. He offered his hand to the older man, and they shook.

"Take care of yourself, brother, and don't forget old Winston here when you are making headway in the real world. I know you won't want to, but if you ever need to come back and talk things through, I ain't never got a queue of people waiting for me on visiting day." Winston smiled and walked away, the prison shadows seeming to consume him as he went.

Moving back to the bed, Declan knew he was ready. He had not been prepared for life in prison, and the education had been swift, but those angry days were behind him. He had dealt with it. The new chapter in his life was starting, and he couldn't wait. Justin had spoken to him, saying that he could stay with his family for a time, until he was at a point where he wanted to or could afford to get his own place.

Despite Declan's plea for Justin to move on with his life, his brother had not listened. He had remained nearby and came to visit his brother every week, sharing every moment of his life with him to the point where it felt as if Declan knew everybody that was going to be out there already.

He couldn't be prouder of his brother and having watched him grow, he never once regretted what he did.

"Howland," the voice of the on-duty officer boomed. "Let's take a walk."

Declan rose from the bed and walked to the door. "Yes, sir," he said with a nod.

The officer, Luke Mollan, had been working at the prison almost as long as Declan had been there. One could even say that they had bonded over the years.

All of the guards knew Declan's story, the real story, and as such, he became one of the prisoners that they could be a little more real with. He was not the only one, not by a long way, but he had also come to think of Luke as something that bordered on being a friend. He was glad that it was him that got to walk him to the gates and not someone else, like Jenkins, the stereotypical prison guard, who loved to torment the prisoners that crossed his path.

They walked through the main rec hall, and a number of inmates walked up and shook Declan's hand or threw him a high five. Others sat in the corners watching and scowling at him; several because of their general dislike for the man, others because of their jealousy at his situation, something they knew they would never have.

Declan looked around one last time at the tight space that had been his home for over half his life. The honest answer was that the thought of the outside world terrified him; the open space, the ability to do whatever he wanted. It was a daunting prospect after being so used to the structure and enclosed space of his cell. The thought of sitting in a room where he could stand up and not touch all four walls without taking more than one small step in any direction was daunting, but he was ready for it.

As they left the main rec hall behind, Declan took one last look over his shoulder as the doors closed, ending the longest, hardest chapter of his life.

They walked through the long corridor, past the visiting hall, the private booths and also the two rooms that had been set up for conjugal visits.

In all of the years, Declan had never noticed that the walls were painted a faded military green color. It was a horrid shade, and he was pretty sure had he noticed it earlier, it would have done nothing to brighten up any occasion that brought him out of general population.

The visitor wing led into the general administration section where officer workers sat dealing with the standard array of paperwork and staff meetings, rarely ever confronting with one of the people they actually worked to maintain. Only on release days such as this, and seeing how Declan was on his own, he didn't believe they would be rushed off their feet with paperwork because of it.

A few raised their eyes to stare at him, but most, he noticed, kept their heads down, focused on their screens, as if raising their heads to look at the visitor they were receiving would somehow cause him to snap and go on some murderous rampage in an effort to have himself hauled back inside. That just wasn't going to happen to him. Nope, he was done and had no intentions of coming back.

With everything signed and sealed, Luke handed Declan an envelope, gave him a hand, which Declan shook, and then he opened the small side door. While it wasn't a magical door in the back of a piece of bedroom furniture, the world he would be taken to when crossing the threshold held the potential to be just as magical.

Taking a deep breath, Declan closed his eyes and said a few silent words of encouragement to himself, and took that final step.

He was free. The sun, the warm breeze, the space around him, it felt as if he had been trapped inside a vacuum and suddenly, the power had been turned off, and the air was rushing back towards him. It was a lot to take in, but he planned on savoring every minute of it.

"Hey there, brother," Justin's voice came from behind him. Declan turned around and saw Justin standing in front of him, and the rush of emotion that slammed into him was enough to make Declan want to weep.

"Hey, man." The two stared at each other for a moment before bursting into matching smiles and embracing with a crushing hug.

"You got old," Justin said as he looked at the grey hair in both Declan's hair and beard.

"Yeah, well, you got … rich, sell-out," Declan replied, punching his brother playfully on the arm.

In the few moments it took to walk over to the car, the brothers laughed and joked and everything felt so normal. Justin couldn't stop smiling, and the nightmare scenarios that had played out in his head the previous seven nights were just that; fantasies of worry, conjured up by a tired brain.

"How does it feel?" Justin asked. "Being free?"

"It feels good. Strange, but good." Declan sat in the passenger seat and stared out of the window. The world had changed, but yet, at the same time, not as much as he had expected. Part of his brain kept telling him that once he got out, the world would be so different he wouldn't recognize it anymore. Finding it to still be a case of blue sky and green grass was almost disappointing.

"Well, you are going to get right back on your feet with us, brother. We are delighted to have you stay, the kids can't wait to meet their uncle, and well …" Justin froze, unsure if the words he was about to say were the right ones. "It's the least I can do."

Spoken quickly, the confidence fell from his words. Justin expected things to become awkward, but Declan looked at him and nodded, changing the subject immediately.

"This thing sure beats the heck out of that old Ford," Declan said, but once again, the words fell flat, and the awkwardness increased, as both brothers recalled how it had been that old Ford that led to the argument in which Declan murdered their abusive father.

They sat in silence for a few moments, Declan content to watch the prison disappear in the rearview mirror and see the countryside spring up around them.

"How far is it to your house?" he asked, looking across at Justin, who was clearly mulling over as many thoughts as Declan was.

"It's about forty-five minutes, give or take. We moved out of the town and into the city first, but when I sold Sav-Tech, we moved back out into the country, kind of in between the two places. It's beautiful there." Justin beamed as he spoke about his house.

"I'm proud of you, brother. You made something of your life, and well, it just, well, you know, it shows me that I did the right thing." The past was something neither man could ever escape, and while both had learned to live with it, living with it together was going to be a whole new experience. They shared a dark bond, and everything that linked them as brothers had been born in a time and place of violence and darkness.

They arrived at the house a little earlier than expected. A large converted farmhouse, not dissimilar to the place owned by Cassie's grandparents all those years previous, it was a three-story property, with the third floor taking up two-thirds of the floor space of the two lower levels. Smoke was rising from the chimney, and the flowerbeds and garden out front were every bit the picture postcard. Two cars were parked in the driveway, a large four-by-four and a truck. The BMW they were in made three.

"Do you have company?" Declan asked, looked at the cars.

"No, they are all ours," Justin said, pulling up beside the truck and shutting off the engine.

Declan got out of the car and stood looking at the vehicles for a few moments, putting off going inside, apprehensive of how things were going to go.

"Here," Justin said, throwing something at his brother.

"Keys?" Declan asked, looking up from the small bundle he held in his hands.

"Yep, two are for the house, back door, and front. The big one is for your new car." Justin patted the truck and smiled at his brother, whose face slowly changed as the realization set in.

"No shit." Declan ran his hands over the hood of the truck, stroking it like a pet.

"Yep, she's all yours, brother. Well, once you get your license again," Justin added.

The door to the house opened and Cassie moved over to her husband, kissing him on the cheek. She had been baking, and the scent of vanilla hung over her like a perfume. It was almost strong enough to hide the aroma of alcohol.

"You're back." Cassie looked over at Declan and smiled. "You must be Declan."

"Yes, ma'am. Thank you for having me. Justin told me everything about you. About how you saved him." Declan walked over and shook Cassie's hand. "Thank you for looking after him."

"Oh, he saved me just as much as I did him. Come on in, I'll show you around." Cassie turned and disappeared into the house.

"She's beautiful, man, well done." Declan slapped his brother on the back and walked inside, chuckling.

Justin watched him go, staying where he was a moment longer, shaken by the strange feeling that was starting to creep over him. He wasn't thinking that it was a mistake to have Declan there, but he just thought it would be, different. The man didn't feel like his brother anymore. Not the way he had back when they were kids.

Justin found Cassie and his brother on the first floor. They had just left the bathroom and were already laughing and joking with one another. It was as if they were old friends, seeing each other for the first time since college, rather than effective strangers meeting for the first time.

Cassie had never visited Declan in prison. It had been Declan's idea. He had not wanted it, saying that first impressions were important and theirs should not be clouded by the consequences of a single moment. Yet, over the years, Justin had opened up to each of them about the other, and so now, talking for the first time, they were coming to realize they were old friends.

"So, our bedroom is here, and the kids took the two on the top floor and this one here," Cassie explained from the hallway, her arms pointing in all different directions. "There are two guest rooms, and either one is yours now. I'd suggest the one at the far end. It's a little bigger, has more natural light, and a great view of the fields out the back."

"Then that one it is. It'll be good to have a view of some wide-open spaces and know I can take a walk in them whenever I feel like it." Declan hoisted his bag onto his shoulders and walked into the room. He had no other belongings than the few possessions he had purchased while inside.

Cassie looked at Justin and smiled. She swayed slightly on her feet and moved after Declan.

Justin stopped her as she walked past. "Hey, is everything alright?" he asked, looking Cassie directly in the eyes.

"Yeah, sure, everything's fine." She smiled again and walked away, pausing in the doorway to the guest bedroom to steady herself.

CHAPTER EIGHT

It had been three weeks since Declan had been released from prison, and he had settled into the family life with ease, picking up the role of doting and protective uncle as if it had been something he had always known.

Despite the tattoos that covered his arms and the neatly trimmed beard that covered his face, he was every bit the softie.

Justin watched his brother interact with his family, and the happy way everybody responded to having him around hurt him to see. It hurt him because the voice of blame was still in his head, whispering to him. It was his fault that Declan did not have a family of his own to love, a new generation made from his blood. There was still time, sure, but since his release, Declan had not left the house much, other than taking a long walk through the fields that surrounded their property. He seemed content with life as a free man, and that only seemed to further compound Justin's guilt, because he knew Declan could do so much better.

Justin graduated not long after Declan had been sentenced, managing to separate this home life from school and from his future life, he passed his exams with flying colors and had his pick of universities.

Studying art and design, he had ambitions to become an illustrator, following the single core passion he had in his life. Midway through his first year, while working on a graphics module, he started to play around with some computer coding and found that designing software was very much like working on his illustrations.

He could take a blank sheet and let his imagination run wild, creating something until it matched his vision. The fact that he was creating software rather than a colorful picture was irrelevant because art was art, and all that was different was the medium used to create.

After sticking with his design course for the rest of his sophomore year, Justin decided to double up on his major, picking up a software development degree also.

He made several things during his first few years, ranging from some simple games to a more complex accounting tool that helped people keep a better record of their financial transactions, coupling in a forecasting tool that would help them analyze the past as a means of looking forward.

The tool had been a huge success, not only earning him his degree but also by becoming the core product of his company, Sav-Tech, which he founded the day of his graduation. He added two more finance tools to his suite, including a cash-handling module and a data transfer tool, which allowed him to capitalize on the surging popularity of the internet and be part of the charge into the new wave of business technology. He eventually sold Sav-Tech for more than enough millions to keep his family and entire bloodline set for a great many generations.

Retiring, he returned to his first love, drawing, and was constantly playing with merging the two, software and art, and while he had nothing that was anywhere near market ready, the surge in AI and computer learning had seen his current prototype come further than he had ever imagined.

His daughters had all inherited his love of art, but one, his middle child, Samantha, was proving to be a wizard when it came to software and understanding the core elements of design. He had even started consulting her. While she was only thirteen, there was a fountain of knowledge in her head that had helped Justin on more than one occasion.

"Uncle Declan, can you help me with this?" Chelsea asked, walking up to her uncle with a homework book in her hands.

Declan had taken a shine to helping the kids with their homework. He said it gave him a chance to kick-start his brain back into gear.

"Of course, pull up a pew and we will take a look." Declan pulled a chair closer to where he was sitting and patted it.

Justin sat and watched them for a little while before getting up from the table and heading outside. Cassie was doing the dishes and watched him leave.

Out on the front porch, Justin pulled out a pack of cigarettes from his jacket pocket and stared at them. He hadn't smoked for many years, and even then, it was never a heavy addiction. Only when something was really bothering him, usually work-related, did he resort to a cheeky smoke and the solitude offered by nature.

The back door creaked, and Justin heard someone moving up behind him. Arms wrapped around his shoulders. "Naughty, naughty," Cassie said, giggling.

"Yeah, I know, but I needed something. I don't know, my head's just all over the fucking place," Justin said, flicking the glowing embers from the end of his smoke.

"What's wrong? Your brother is great, and he has settled right into the family." Cassie dropped her embrace and scooted down next to Justin on the rear steps.

"That's just it." Justin paused, taking a deep breath, looking over his shoulder to check that nobody could overhear their conversation. "He's settled in great, with all of you, but me ... I don't know. Like I said, my head's a mess and I just need to sort my shit out."

"Talk to me." Cassie put her hand on her husband's shoulder, rubbing it in a one-handed massage.

"That's just it. I don' know what to say. It's just different to what I expected. I look inside and he's doing so well, but it just doesn't feel like it's my brother sitting there." Justin looked at the cigarette burning in his hands, and suddenly, the taste was gone. With a quiet grunt of dissatisfaction, he tossed it through the air and onto the drive below. The damp ground extinguished the orange embers, slowly drowning each one, the orange glow fading like a sun setting on yet another fading habit.

"Don't be so hard on yourself. It's going to take some getting used to," Cassie said as she rubbed her hands together.

"I guess. It's just, we've not spent more than ten minutes together since he got out, and when we do, there's just this silence between us. I don't know, it just feels awkward." Justin knew he was sounding like a whiny brat, but he had waited so long to get his brother back, and now, it just felt as though he was still waiting.

"Then talk to him about it," Cassie said, still rubbing her hands together.

"Cold?" Justin asked, noticing the new tick for the first time.

"Yeah, I just can't get warm recently. I think a drink will help warm me up." She stood up and kissed Justin on the top of his head. "Talk to your brother, sort it out, and if you're lucky, you can sort me out too."

Justin knew what that meant. His wife was planning on getting so wasted she would jump him like a horny teenager by the time he came bed. He wasn't going to complain; drunk sex always meant Cassie went a little bit wild.

Turning to watch her walk away, he saw Declan standing in the doorway. He was watching his brother, a sadness in his eyes breaking through from the chest where he kept them buried.

"Hey, brother," he said, not moving from the door.

"Hey," Justin replied feeling nervous, and guilty. He chided himself for feeling so bad.

"So ..." Declan stepped forward, and for a second, Justin thought he was going to sit down beside him the same Cassie had done.

Declan carried on, walking down the steps and out into the field that fed directly from the rear the house.

"It's a nice night, isn't it?" Declan asked, looking up at the stars, the darkness all but swallowing him.

"It's a beauty, that's for sure," Justin said, getting up from the step.

"I'm sorry," Declan spoke, turning his back on his brother to look down the field and into the void that lay beyond. Declan had grown fond of the darkness, finding a comfort he had never noticed before in the endlessness of it. When everything around you turned to black, then there were no walls to your cage, and the only thing holding you back was your own perception of where you were.

"Sorry for what?" Justin asked, moving down to stand beside his brother.

"For everything. For coming here." Declan let out a sigh.

"How much did you hear?" Justin asked, feeling the same awkwardness building between them.

"Enough," Declan turned, and his eyes glistened in the dark, wet with tears.

"Listen, I'm sorry, I just ... I –"

"I get it. You're not lying, don't worry. I feel it too. It's like we are strangers to one another," Declan said, cutting his brother off.

"Exactly. I want you here, Dec, I want you in my life and as part of my family, but I want my brother back too." Justin felt the surge of emotion hit him but refused to let himself cry.

"We are still brothers, it's just that a lot of crap has gone on over the years, and well, we just need to gather the pieces again." Declan stepped forward, his hand suddenly raised. "Don't move."

Reaching out, he quickly grabbed something from Justin's shoulder and threw it into the night. "Bug," he said. "I know how much you don't like them."

Justin took a step back. "That's exactly it. You know I never used to like them, but I faced that fear a while back while processing everything that happened. I'm good with bugs now. There's even a photo somewhere of me holding a tarantula."

"Oh, sorry, I just figured ..." Declan stammered, lowering his eyes to the floor. "It's strange, isn't it, how you can live with someone for so long, and still feel like strangers?"

"I think that's the problem. I think that's why it's so easy with Cassie and the kids." Justin felt himself loosen up, spurred on by the admission that his brother felt it too.

"What is?" Declan looked up.

"Because to them, you are a stranger. It's the first time you have met them, they don't know anything. But with us, we know each other, we know the darkest secrets and have lived through more than most people should ever have to know about." Justin felt as if he was raising his voice, but Declan gave no indication that he needed to calm down.

"So, you're saying it's always going to be like this?" Declan asked.

"No, just, well, we are not the same people we were back then. We have the same history, and the same secrets, but who we are now, is not who we were then. Me, I've changed. With the fear of bugs, and being able to talk about mum and dad without cramping up in fear that they would come running if I said their name too loud. You, I mean, you went to prison, for me. You sacrificed your entire life, and that is on me." While Justin had started off with one plan in his mind, his heart had taken over, and the words were flowing with no sign of being tamed.

"What are you talking about, bro? You're not to blame." Declan paused for a second, before stepping closer to his brother. Justin flinched, not in fear, but because he wasn't ready yet. There was still more to say.

"Like hell I'm not! You killed dad for what he was doing to me, and that changed your life forever. I see you in there, with the kids, and with us, laughing and joking and it is killing me to know I took away your chance at having all that." The tears were flowing now, scalding tears, the likes of which Justin hadn't felt for many years. "I can't take that back, and you should hate me for having what I have."

"Hate you? That's insane. You're my brother, I am proud of what you have accomplished. You worked hard and changed your life around." Declan's eyes were filled with tears.

"That might be, but it cost you yours." Now Justin was shouting.

"No," Declan argued, his voice loud, but more with a plea than with anger.

"Why don't you hate me?" Justin yelled, feeling the walls inside his mind crumble as the emotions overflowed.

His head pounded and spittle flew from his lips in thick stands as he wept before his brother.

"You should resent me." Justin dropped to his knees.

"I love you. You're my baby brother, and I'm just sorry you had to live with what you did, for so long. It should be me asking you for forgiveness." Declan took hold of Justin and hauled him to his feet, pulling him into a bear hug, squeezing him so tightly that Justin couldn't breathe. His bones ached from the force of the embrace, but neither man wanted to let go.

Both men were weeping, finding support in the other as much as they looked to offer it in return.

"Daddy?" Chelsea was standing in the kitchen doorway, the lights of the house burning behind her.

"Yes, honey?" Justin asked, wiping his eyes as he tried to regain his composure.

"Is everything okay? Why are you yelling?" Her voice was timid, unused to raised voices.

"I'm not yelling, sweetie, me and your uncle Declan were just talking, that's all. I guess we got a little carried away." Justin felt his brother close to him, a strong hand on resting on his shoulder.

"Are you sure?" Chelsea asked, her inquisitive nature shining through.

"I'm sure, honey. Go on inside and ask your sister to make you some cocoa, it's almost time for bed." Justin's voice had regained its normal composure, and Chelsea accepted his answer without any further questions.

"Thank you," Justin said to his brother, without turning around.

"No sweat, that's what big brothers are for," Declan answered, his hand disappearing from his brother's shoulder. "I think I'm going to hang around out here for a little while longer."

Justin walked inside, feeling better about himself that he had in days. A weight had been lifted from his shoulders, and he felt as if he could breathe again. He was sure that he would sleep like a baby once he got to bed.

The kids had dispersed from the kitchen, heading to their rooms. They had a bedtime, and they stuck to it well. They each had a TV in their room, and often Tammy, their eldest, would usually watch TV until late, which was fine, just not on school nights.

Justin checked everything was turned off and slid into the bedroom. Cassie was asleep, stretched diagonally across the bed, the bottle of wine on the bedside table all but empty. The empty glass laid on its side on the bedside table, down like a king piece on the chessboard, a sign of her surrender to the day, and to the demons of yesterday.

Justin took hold of his wife and rolled her over, her skirt riding up to reveal her lack of underwear. "I'm all yours," she slurred to Justin, wrapping her arms around him.

"No, not tonight." He tried to break her embrace. "You've had too much,"

Cassie's eyes snapped open, blazing with a fiery anger. "Oh, there we go again. Cassie, you drink too much. Cassie has a problem." She tried to roll away from him and only succeeded in falling from the bed.

"Honey, are you alright?" Justin asked, moving to stand.

Cassie's head appeared, and a goofy laugh escaped her. "Well, maybe this time you're right. I've had like one too many, just one. A little bit."

She laughed as she pushed herself to her feet, ripping open her blouse, sending buttons flying in all directions, their impact sounding like hailstones as they pinged off the wall, and the wine bottle, which gave a near musical clink. "Take me, baby."

Cassie fell on her husband, wearing only her bra, and while Justin wanted to refuse, his body had other ideas. He just hoped that Cassie wouldn't wake the kids, as she was not a quiet lover when drunk.

CHAPTER NINE

Justin was awake long before Cassie. Rising, he showered and shaved, getting himself ready for the day. He was careful not to make too much noise but also knew that after a night like the previous one, Cassie would sleep through a tornado and wake up without a clue of anything having occurred while she slept.

As he left the room, Justin made sure to cover up her naked body. His wife usually only ever slept in the nude, but had a habit of losing the bedcovers too. He didn't want the kids, or his brother, walking in and seeing her like that.

Once he was confident that what remained of her dignity was safely tucked away under the musical note-themed duvet cover, he turned and headed downstairs.

The kids were already down, and Tammy had made them all some cereal. They were sitting at the table in the kitchen, watching cartoons on the medium-sized TV that hung on the wall.

"Morning, guys, any plans for the day?" Justin asked as he flicked on the coffee maker, chiding himself at forgetting to set the timer. Grabbing a bottle of water while he waited, he stole a piece of toast from the table and waited for an answer.

"I'm heading out with Mary and Tina," Tammy said, turning her head from the TV. "We're heading to the mall to catch a movie. Can I have some money?"

Tammy knew her father was a pushover, but batted her eyelids at him anyway.

"Sure thing," Justin said, swapping the coffee pot out for a cup, unwilling to wait any longer for his morning jolt.

"What about you two? Any crazy adventures planned?"

Chelsea giggled. "Uncle Declan was going to take us for a walk through the woods. I want to collect some pine cones."

"Sounds like fun, can I tag along?" Justin asked, eager to spend some more time with his brother.

He had laid awake the night before, still unable to turn his mind off, even after he and Cassie had undoubtedly woken the neighbors. He'd had an idea that, as usual, arrived just before he fell asleep, the sudden clarity finally allowing his mind the peace and quiet it needed to shut down. He just needed to suggest it.

Declan came downstairs an hour later, his hair ruffled by sleep and a strand of cotton stuck to his beard. The girls giggled, and Chelsea took great pleasure in pulling it free. "It looks like a spider made a web in your beard, Uncle Declan."

"Thank goodness you caught it early then," Declan said, ruffling the top of her head. "Morning, brother. Is the coffee ready?"

"Sure is, made it good and strong," Justin said, moving to one side to let Declan get at the things he needed.

"Yeah, I imagine you need to get your energy levels back up and running this morning." Declan winked at his brother, and Justin felt his face turn red immediately. The heat radiated from him. "Don't worry, it's a good thing you still can still make that much noise together."

Declan spoke under his breath so the kids wouldn't hear and punched his brother on the arm, just as he used to do when they were kids.

"Hey, man, I was thinking. Why don't you and I take a trip together?" Justin turned to face his brother, setting his coffee mug onto the side.

"You mean like go shopping or something? I do need to expand my wardrobe a little." Declan looked down at the Zeppelin T-shirt that he was wearing.

"No, I mean a real trip. Get away from every for a few days. Just the two of us. We could go do something fun," Justin suggested.

"You mean like camping or something?" Declan's eyes turned toward the ceiling and he started nodding his head.

"Something like that, sure. There's plenty of cool places, and we could do some things while we are there, you know, like bonding things." Justin felt a little silly talking in such terms, but he wanted to have a relationship with his brother, and that meant they needed to start a new one together.

"You mean like rafting and hiking some crazy trails, build up a new set of memories with us as the people we are now?" Declan continued to nod his head as he talked, the idea not only growing on him but consuming his mind.

"Exactly." Justin smiled.

"That's a great idea. Get away, just the two of us, we can have some drinks, have some adventures. I'm sold. When do we leave? I'm a very light packer these days." Declan smiled and took a big gulp of coffee. "Do you guys have any bacon left?"

Declan made a fried breakfast for him and his brother, making sure he made enough bacon for the kids too because even while they all said they didn't want anything, three sets of eyes watched the crispy bacon rashers with mouth-watering interest.

"There's some in the pan still," Declan said without looking at the kids, almost as an aside, dropping a subtle hint for them to follow.

The sound of scraping chairs rang out as all three hurried over to the pan.

"Hey, that pan is hot, let Tammy dish it all up for you," Justin added as he burst the yolk of his egg, stabbing it with a bacon spear.

"Tam, you mind if Declan and I tag along on the way to the mall? We can take my car and we'll either come pick you up later or just wait for you and we can drive back together," Justin spoke, as he finished his breakfast and sat back from the table. "Before you roll your eyes or anything, I promise we won't cramp your style or anything."

"Ugh," Tammy said, rolling her eyes, not at the suggestion, but at her father's continued insistence that he had even the vaguest understanding of what was cool.

"I'll take that as a yes," Justin said as he cleared that table.

It was already ten-thirty, and there was no sign of Cassie. Justin pondered going to wake her but thought better of it. Let her sleep it off.

While the kids got ready, Declan did the dishes, something he insisted on doing by hand, rather than using the machine. Justin took the moment and disappeared into his office to tidy up a few things he needed to get squared away. While he was there, he browsed the net for some possible camping locations where he and Declan could go. He also wrote Cassie a note so that when she woke up, she wouldn't panic at being alone.

With the note left beside the bed, swapping it out for the wine bottle and glass, the kids ready and the emails he needed to do all typed up and sent, the family bundled into the car and were off.

The peril of taking the two younger kids with them meant it became a trip that involved spending a lot of time in both the bookstore and the toy store, and when they finally made it to a clothes shop, the items they were looking at were not suitable for grown men at all, and thankfully not available in any sizes that came close to fitting.

"Would you look at this ugly thing?" Justin said, picking up a giant stuffed spider toy. Its body was the size of a football, with eight hairy legs and a set of thick black fangs curving down from its mouth.

"It's a stuffed monstrosity," Declan said, pretending to shiver at the sight of the toy.

"There's more of them, look." Justin moved around the display case and saw three more giant bug toys. A scorpion, a millipede, or centipede, the number of legs was completely disproportionate for either creature, so identification was impossible. The last toy was a strange-looking creature that appeared to be a mix between a spider and a crab, with long pincers that seemed to fold inwards on themselves via an elbow joint. Picking up the toy, Justin pulled on the pincer and it extended, showing two rows of fluffy teeth.

"Who in the world would buy this stuff for their kids?" Declan asked, staring at the pile of bug dolls.

"And for this price too. Look." Justin held up the price tag.

"Fuck me," Declan said a little too loud. "Sorry," he said to the young mother standing close by, a toddler pulling at her leggings with one hand, while his other clutched some sort of car, which clearly held great meaning and importance in his life.

"I'm happy for them to stay that price as long as they don't get that big in real life," Justin said, returning the weird creature to the pile. "I can cope with most bugs now, but something like that? Hell no."

"Toys sure have changed a since I was a kid," Declan said as they walked out of the shop and leaned against the railing of the third-floor shopping level.

Behind them was a drop down into a large water feature, which served as the central meeting point for the mall. Inside, they could see Chelsea and her sister Rebecca looking around the shelves, trying hard to decide what one thing they were going to get, while both making no attempt to hide the fact they each already had one item and were looking for a second.

"They know you're a pushover, don't they?" Declan said, laughing.

"Oh yeah, that's why they come here with me and not their mum," Justin said.

The kids waved their dad down when they were ready, and each managed to convince him to buy two things each. Once they had rung up the total, Justin went to put everything in the car, while Declan took the girls to the food court.

He met them just in time to place his order. They ate their food and chatted, trying to come to a shared consensus over the film they wanted to see. Declan jokingly suggested a horror movie, to which Rebecca was worryingly quick to agree to. Justin wanted an action movie, joining in on the fun, and ultimately, they ended up at the latest Pixar release with talking machines and a storyline that was stronger than most other movies Justin had seen in recent times.

They returned home with a car filled with things, including a lot of stuff for Declan, who had been hesitant to abuse his brother's bank card at first but eventually came to realize that there were a lot of essentials that he still didn't own.

Cassie was waiting for them, busy cooking a large roast dinner. Having had the house to herself most of the day, she had cleaned, tidied, and cooked. It was her idea of heaven, and her good mood reflected the day she had had.

"I think that's a wonderful idea," she said that evening as Justin suggested his trip idea to her. "You too could do with some time together."

"Have you given any thought as to where?" Declan asked as he drank his beer and watched the game on television. Not a huge sports fan, he could watch anything and find enjoyment in it.

"There are a few places close by, and a couple a little further away. One place seems really cool. It's a short flight from here, but there is rafting, hiking trails, and a big cave system that you can get walking tours through," Justin said, reeling off the information he had seen online. "Remember how much we used to talk about going camping, back when we were kids?"

"Yeah, man that always seemed like fun. Campfires, marshmallows, and ghost stories," Declan replied, giving a little laugh at the end.

"Exactly. I figured what a better way to start something new than by taking a trip we had always wanted to take when we were younger." Justin looked across at his brother, who nodded his head before he spoke his reply.

"That sounds cool. When would you want to go?" Declan asked. "I mean, I'm free whenever. I don't have any pending job applications right now. I got rejected from everything in the last round of things I sent off."

"Whenever we can get it booked, I guess," Justin answered.

"Well, let's take a closer look tomorrow and see what works. I don't want to get in the way of your home life," Declan said with a yawn and a stretch. "I think I'm going to turn in for the night. Have a good one, brother."

"Night, bro."

With the room to themselves, Justin and Cassie curled up on the sofa and channel surfed until they were both almost too sleepy to make it upstairs and into bed.

CHAPTER TEN

Justin pushed the last bag into the back of the car and checked that everything was securely fastened in. Only then did he close the rear door, giving it an extra push for good measure, as if there were different levels of being closed.

"Are you sure you have everything?" Cassie asked. She had stood, watching the brothers load the car for the past forty-five minutes, enjoying watching them work as a team to get everything organized. Both seemed genuinely happy and excited about their trip.

In the two weeks since their argument in the backyard, their relationship had moved from strength to strength.

"We've got more than enough. We're camping after all. I doubt we will even get to use half the stuff we have packed." Justin said, walking back towards the house.

He kissed Cassie on the forehead and once more on the lips. "Are you going to be okay?" It had been a long time since he had left Cassie alone for any period of time, and it was something he did not do lightly.

Her drinking had eased a little in recent weeks, but she was still drinking something every day. He worried that with the kids old enough to look after themselves, for the most part, that she would go off the rails the way she had back before they got married.

"I'll be fine. Just don't go falling off any cliffs or getting lost in the caves." Cassie smiled, but she couldn't hide the sadness in her eyes.

"I promise not to get eaten by any giant bugs or anything like that." Justin smiled, heading back to the car where Declan sat in the passenger seat, leaning over to sound the horn in mock irritation.

Pulling away, Justin waved his arm out of the window while Declan arranged the playlist. They weren't even out of the driveway before Sweet Child of Mine was blasting out of the speakers, and the brothers were singing along even more off-key than Axl acting as a stand in vocal for AC/DC.

The drive took them two days, with a stop at a cheap hotel the first night. Justin had the money to pay for flights, but both agreed the fun was in the entire journey, and a road trip would be much more entertaining. It was the same reason why they chose a cheap motel above anything more expensive. If they were going to be roughing it in a tent, then they needed to start things properly. Although five minutes after closing the door to their shared room, both were questioning their decision, as the room was clearly overpriced. The mold on the walls was thicker than the carpet, and it was hard to find a clean spot on the bedding to lie down. All it took was a single look at the bathroom for them to gather their things and sleep in the car, laughing already at the stories they would be able to tell once they got home.

It was a cold night so the brothers cracked open their sleeping bags to keep warm. It must have been quite a sight for anybody that happened past, to gaze in and see what could only be likened to two dead bodies, packaged up and ready for dumping.

They woke early the next morning and decided to skip a trip to the breakfast room that the motel so proudly boasted about on their advertising board, settling instead for a drive-through meal somewhere close to midmorning.

The early start meant they were early to the park and had all the time to pick the perfect location to pitch their tent. The trip was planned out with enough to keep them busy for the week, and they were planning on pitching up at four different locations through the park, giving them the perfect opportunity to try out the full range of activities.

Their first spot was higher up in the hills that was just failing to qualify as mountains, although they would become them half a state to the north. They had two different cave tours planned, the first one of which held the honor of being the number one tourist attraction in the state. They then had two days of hiking before they moved on to their second spot.

It was mid-afternoon before they saw anybody else arrive, and by early evening, there was only more tent added to the group.

Introductions were short, with Justin and Declan letting the others come to them, not feeling overly inclined to bond with strangers when the goal of the trip was to spend time together.

The other tent had two men that could only be described as hipsters, and who, at first glance, seemed far removed from their natural environment. It surprised the brothers how easily one of the pair put their tent together. After introductions were made, it transpired that one of the two was an experienced camper who had been staying in the park since childhood. His partner was very much the man who went camping to keep his other half happy, rather than as a result of any natural inclination on his part.

They were a friendly couple and had brought beers with them, which certainly went some way to break the ice.

"So, you are really telling me, that this man right there, your brother, is the CEO of Sav-Tech?" the non-camping hipster asked.

"The former CEO," Justin corrected them as he sat back down around their campfire. "I sold everything a while ago."

"Hey, where did you go to take a piss?" Declan asked.

"Just behind the camp there. I walked about a hundred meters behind the tents, found a good tree, and just let it flow," Justin said, laughing. While not quite drunk, each man had a good buzz going.

"I'll be right back then." Declan clapped his brother on the shoulder as he stood and walked away.

"So what do you do now?" Trevor, the non-camping hipster, asked.

"I'm working on a few things, but technically I've retired already. I loved working in tech, but I love enjoying life even more." Justin looked around as if needed to soak up the dark scene around them.

"Lucky bastard," Ben, the other hipster, said, resting back against his back to gaze up at the stars.

"It is beautiful out here," he said both to the group and to nobody in particular.

"I've never been a big fan of the outdoors," Trevor said. "However, I know you love it, and I love you." The pair smiled at each other when suddenly the sound of something scurrying through the woods broke up their moment.

"What was that?" Trevor asked, jumping.

"Probably just a small animal or something," Ben replied, looking over at his partner. "Don't worry, you're not going to get attacked by a bear or anything."

"I'm not worried about that, but you have to admit, that noise was too close and too large for it to be some small critter." Trevor was instantly uncomfortable, and from the look on his face in the dancing light of the flames, it would take a lot to bring him back down.

"Maybe it was another camper arriving, or Declan getting lost. He does that from time to time," Justin said, trying to offer alternative suggestions.

"I do what?" Declan asked, rejoining the group.

"What, oh, nothing. Something was scurrying around out there, that's all. We told Trevor that it might be you." Justin drained the rest of his beer and threw the can into the plastic bag they had set up as a bin.

"Wasn't me, but hey, I did see the other campers. They are further down in the hills. Guess they got here late and didn't want to hike up or anything." Declan pointed away from their camp, not that anybody could see anything in the darkness.

"Really, that's strange. The books all recommend getting up high." Justin cocked his head.

"Maybe they are high, and we're just higher," Declan joked. "But there are about six or seven tents down there and a few campfires too. Maybe we better head down tomorrow morning, early, and then we can all hike back up together."

"I bet someone local is part of their group," Ben said.

"Why would that make a difference?" Justin asked, cocking his head.

"Well, locals know this place, know its history. They probably told them the Crawleigh ghost story and got them all scared." Ben looked around as if checking the darkness to make sure they were alone.

"Oh God, don't start with that," Trevor groaned, clearly well-accustomed to hearing the tale.

"Nah, it's cool. I could go for a ghost story," Declan said, sitting upright on the log, holding his hands out towards the fire.

"Well, the legend goes back to the founding families, who created a settlement out here by the name of Crawleigh," Ben started, sliding onto the ground, settling down with his back against the log. "The settlement grew fast, and everybody that arrived prospered. Nobody knew why, but everything just fell into place, and the town grew and grew. Then one day, a little boy went missing. It was the first bad thing to happen in the settlement. They never found him, and then, six months later, another kid disappeared, and then another. Word spread to the other settlements in the area, which unlike Crawleigh, had struggled to find their footing. Disease, crime, you name it, it was rife, and everybody started pointing fingers at those they thought responsible.

"There were witch hunts and lynch mobs, people were executed on sight for their perceived involvement in the disappearances. Things settled down for a while, but then one day, a year to the day since the last disappearance, another child went missing. Now, this is where the story gets weird because there's a couple of versions. Some say that the father, a widower after his wife died in childbirth, was lead to the body by the ghost of his son. Others say that the child's screams rang out so loud that the entire township was drawn from their beds. Either way, the father of the missing boy took his buddies and led them straight to the mayor's house. In his basement, they found all of the bodies. But that wasn't everything. He had all manner of images and icons drawn onto the walls, in blood, and books about witchcraft and sacrifices.

"It didn't take long for everybody in the mayor's group to be hunted down. People wanted them hanged, but instead, they were banished, driven into the mountains, forced to live out the rest of their days in hiding, shunned by Crawleigh and the surrounding communities. The town changed its name, and while it prospered, it also knew dark times; times of famine and sickness. Some people still claim that the descendants of those Crawleigh natives are still living out here, roaming the woods, looking for victims. They live in the caves, beneath them, hiding by day and only coming out once it was dark."

Ben stopped talking and looked at the brothers. He had told the story with such seriousness and fervor, but now it was done, the laugh was forcing its way to the surface.

All four men broke down, laughing at the tale as the campfire flames twisted and danced in front of them, and the darkness lay in wait, circling them, and drawing ever closer.

"That's a cool story," Declan said. "Little original in places, but you get a good grade for the effort you put in."

"Yeah, he loves that story. Pulls it out every chance he gets," Trevor said, putting his hand on Ben's shoulder.

"It's a cool story, and the kids always love it when we do campouts with the church," Ben jokingly defended himself.

"Well, what can top off a night of good company better than a campfire ghost story," Justin said, yawning. Ben nodded and pointed to Justin to show the others that at least one of the group understood it. "I'm going to turn in before it gets so late that the morning is already here." Justin stood up and stretched.

"I'll join you," Declan agreed, draining his beer in one long pull. He was unable to stifle the belch that came thereafter, but nobody seemed to take offense.

As the brothers got into their tent, Trevor and Ben sat together finishing their drinks. They had promised to put out the fire before they turned in, and at least Ben had the experience to know how to do it. They had a bucket of dirt ready to pour onto the flames and had stopped feeding the pile a while before, letting it die down naturally for a while.

Inside the tent, away from the fire, it was cool, but still a nice temperature. The brothers slid into the sleeping bags and without the need to chat further, both fell asleep. The flames of the dwindling fire dancing on the walls of the tent like a child's mobile, giving their brains something relaxing to focus on as sleep claimed them.

Justin woke first in the morning and lay in the bag, enjoying the warmth. Declan woke a short time later, sitting up and stretching before getting out of the bag without hesitation.

"Be right back, got to take care of the morning ritual." He disappeared from the tent and came back a few minutes later with a confused look on his face.

"What's up?" Justin asked. He was up and dressed and packing up his gear when Declan returned.

"Those guys from last night, what was it, Ben and Trevor?" Declan said.

"Yeah, what about them?" Justin looked at his brother.

"They've gone"

"Gone? Gone how?" Justin pulled the strings on his back and secured his sleeping bag against it.

"Gone as in, their tent is still there, but there's no sign of them." Declan started working on packing his gear. "I mean, they probably just set out down to the others, but I thought we were going to head down together."

"Maybe they were up early and decided to get a headstart," Justin said, unconcerned.

"Maybe, but it just seems strange. They were cool guys, and then they just bug out on us." Declan shook the thought away and finished packing up his things. "Oh well, shall we grab a bite to eat and then head down, or just eat something quick on the go?"

"Well, let's head down and make some introductions. We can eat a power bar or something on the way," Justin said.

"Sounds delicious," Declan teased.

"Asshole," Justin shot back, smiling.

It didn't take them long to get everything packed away, taking the decision to move their camp down to the others. They didn't want to appear antisocial in any way.

"Do you feel that?" Declan asked as they walked down a steep and clearly seldom-used pathway. It was hard to see it in certain places, where the forest had reclaimed it as its own.

"Feel what?" Justin asked, sweat coating his forehead.

"I don't know, just kind of feels like we are being watched. I thought I saw somebody move through the trees, like a kid or something." Declan stopped to take a drink of water.

"A kid?" Justin looked back at his brother.

"Yeah, I mean, it was small, you know, kid-sized," Declan puffed out and replaced the bottle in his pack. "Are you sure we're going the right way? This path is looking pretty unpathlike."

"It was probably just a kid. This is a popular hiking and camping spot. There's bound to be a lot of others out here too," Justin said, unconcerned. "And yes, I'm sure this is the way."

Declan followed without argument, pushing through the plants and ferns, his eyes constantly on the trees, where he just knew someone was still watching them. *Stupid kids.*

A few meters further down, after the ground took a sharp and sudden downturn, they came to a point of lower vegetation and saw the path they should have been following appear to their immediate right. Declan didn't need to say anything before Justin turned around and gave him a grin.

"Hey, I got us here at least, and we were heading in the right direction." Moving over to the path, the going became that much easier.

Declan also noticed that the kids that had been following them had also disappeared. It was not as easy to scare someone when they were walking along a trail, rather than forcing their path through the woods.

"I see the others. They are all packed up and look ready to leave," Justin said as they came to a crossroads on the trail.

They reached the group before they left and were greeted by several surprised faces. The previous evening had been spent getting to know one another, and now a group was arriving late to the party. It threw off the dynamic and earned the brothers a number of slightly hostile looks.

"Sorry, we're late. We camped higher up," Justin said as he dropped his pack and wiped the sweat from his brow. It was still early, but the temperature was getting up, and the trek through the woods had not been an easy one.

"Higher up?" a man in full bush-gear asked. He had a name badge that claimed he was called Tim and that he worked for the park.

"Yeah, my brother and I. We arrived early yesterday and hiked up into the hills a little bit more. We camped there with these other guys. Have they not arrived yet?" Justin looked around, expecting to see Trevor and Ben standing among the group.

"Nobody has joined us since last night," a heavy-set man with a thick grey beard answered. "Mitch and his wife there were the last ones to arrive."

"Oh, that's strange. They left well before us. I mean, they were already gone when we woke up. I'm Justin, by the way, and this is my brother Declan." Both men offered a hand to the bearded man, who took them in a meaty grip and gave a firm shake.

"I'm Zeke, and that right there is my wife, Tilly. I'll let the others introduce themselves and all, but that's who we are." Zeke was a friendly man, contrary to the gruff exterior that was not aided by the rotting skull he had emblazoned across this shirt.

"How high up did you camp?" Tim asked, peering at the pair.

"I don't know, um ..." Justin turned, looking back up the side of the hills, trying to find the spot they had made camp. "I guess that ledge up there was close to where we were. We pitched up a way back from the edge."

Tim moved over to where Justin and Declan were standing, looking from them, up into the hills and back to them once more before taking a slow breath ahead of speaking. "You say there were two others with you?"

"Yeah, a couple of guys, kind of hipster-looking, but they were cool," Declan answered. "I expected them to be down here by now."

"Well, we will wait a few more minutes, there's enough time," the park ranger spoke, his gaze set on the ledge above.

Declan raised his head to try and see what was holding the man's attention so much that it distracted his voice, but saw nothing. Then something moved, disappearing from the edge before his brain had even realized it was there. All he knew was that something had gone.

"Was that them?" he asked, looking at the ranger.

Tim looked at Declan but said nothing. "I need to make a phone call," he spoke slowly, as if hesitant for something. "Once I get back, we will head off. If those guys aren't here, that's their loss. It's a 45-minute hike up to the caves, and I don't want to shortchange you all on your time underground."

Declan watched the ranger walk away, and how he threw another glance up into the hills before grabbing the radio from his belt. Turning to talk to his brother, Declan found himself alone. Justin had joined the group and was busy being introduced to the others.

"Guys, this is my brother, Declan. Declan, this is Joe, Becky, and Tara," Justin said, leading the introductions, and Declan shook hands with the three people.

"Nice to meet you," Declan said, smiling at Tara in particular.

At average height with short-cut brown hair and dark brown eyes, it was her caramel complexion that made Declan pause for more. He guessed she was of an Indonesian descent.

"Nice to meet you too. Are you looking forward to the caves?" Tara asked, her voice still holding a trace of an accent that made her words sound that much sweeter to Declan's ears

"Yeah, I can't wait. I've never been in a cave before," Declan said, his eyes not moving to the others.

"Me neither. I'm hoping it's not too cramped. I'm not a big fan of small spaces," Tara said as she shifted her weight from one foot to the other every few seconds.

"You get used to them," Declan replied without thinking.

"What do you mean?" Tara asked.

"Nothing, I just mean, I've spent a lot of my time in confined spaces, and you get used to them," Declan answered, trying to think of a follow-up statement and avoid having to bring up the whole prison, murder charge subject.

"Oh, yeah I guess you do." Tara gave a laugh and took Declan by the hand, leading him away from the group.

"Well, that didn't take long," Becky said, her words a little too curt to be coming from anything but bad experiences.

"It could be a record," Joe said in agreement.

"She does that more often then?" Justin asked, unsure how well the three knew each other.

"As long as I have known her. Too nice for her own good," Becky said, her irritation clear.

"She's naïve, that's all," Joe said, trying to keep things more civil.

"Well, don't worry. I can vouch for my brother. He's one of the good ones," Justin said, feeling overcome by the sudden urge to be elsewhere.

Looking around, he spotted Zeke and his wife, a petite older lady who wore a pair of jeans, a pale pink checkered blouse, and a pair of cowboy boots. They were talking to another couple and gave Justin the exit he needed.

"Excuse me, I'm going to introduce myself to the others," Justin said, leaving Joe and Becky, who were watching Declan and their friend like a pair of hawks.

Zeke was a warm and welcoming man, with a character even larger than his gut. Justin stood with him and his wife until the ranger returned, the worried look seemingly set onto his face. As the man started to speak, barking out instructions, Justin looked around for his brother. Declan had disengaged from his conversation with Tara, who herself had wandered back to rejoin her friends.

"That looked like it was going well," Justin teased his brother.

"You'd think, wouldn't you? She got the face of an angel, but talk to her for a few minutes and you will see she's a devil," Declan said with a strong sigh.

"Really? She looks so sweet." Justin said.

"Yep, but trust me, she's got bat-shit crazy written all over her. I'm staying well away." Declan turned to face the ranger, putting Tara firmly behind him.

"Sorry about the late start, but sometimes the day job still needs to take preference," Tim spoke, raising his voice so that everybody could hear. "We've got about a 45-minute hike up to the caves, an hour at most, so we'll still have plenty of time, but I'm going to ask you all to stay on the trail. Don't go wandering off or looking at the scenery. There's plenty of time for that later on." The group nodded with various degrees of enthusiasm, but Declan heard the words that were not being spoken.

A chill ran down his spine, and a voice in his head whispered that something was wrong. He laughed it off, cracking a joke with his brother, but as they started to walk, he could not stop from looking deeper into the woods on both sides, expecting to find something standing there, ready to snatch anybody that did not heed the ranger's warning.

The hike started off easy going one, the train well-worn and carefully chosen. There were several other trails that spawned from theirs, but their pathway was a far steeper one. The only member of the group that showed any sign of exertion was Zeke, but his infectious laugh and unashamed self-deprecating wit carried him through.

By the time they arrived at the cave, they were all sweating. It was unusually hot, and the trees only served to capture the heat and amplify it like a natural sauna, which only served to charge the group's eagerness to enter the cave, if not only because it would be so much cooler.

The park ranger led them inside, stopping just beneath the cover of the rock but before the darkness grew too much for everybody to be able to see him clearly.

"That's better," he said, wiping the sweat from his forehead. "Now, this is the main entrance to the cave system. There are others, but this one gives us the best route and the best views and takes us through the main cavern, where you will be able to see the natural spring that rises up. I'm sure most of you have seen the bottles of water in the store, the one with the shield logo." Everybody nodded. "Well, that comes from this spring. Not this exact spot, but they share the same source. You will all be allowed to fill one bottle or water canister from the spring." The ranger continued giving the instructions, but Declan found himself watching the walls of the cave, checking to make sure everything was alright.

He didn't want to say it to Justin, but the walls were feeling pretty tight around him, and he was still unable to shake the feeling of unease that was surging through his body.

"So, if you all want to grab a helmet from the rack over here, we can get going. I'll warn you, it can get a little cramped in places, but nothing that this group can't handle. I want you all to keep an orderly line. We will stop regularly to take photos, and I will point out the key areas as we go, but please remember, do not fall behind. The walkways are marked and roped off, but nobody wants to get lost in the caves, especially not since what happened to the last family." The ranger paused for a moment before breaking out into a grin. "Just kidding, we've never lost anybody yet."

The group gave a laugh, all except Declan, who felt more on edge. He stared at the park ranger, and when the man's eyes locked on his, it was the ranger that quickly averted his gaze.

"Hey, man, do you think there's something he's not telling us?" Declan whispered to his brother while the pair grabbed the helmets and strapped them into place.

"What are you talking about?" Justin looked at his brother with no clue as to what he was talking about.

"I mean Trevor and Ben. Didn't you see his reaction when we told him about where we camped? I'm sure I saw something move up on the ledge where we were." Declan tried not to sound like a loon as he spoke and made an extra effort to keep his voice a whisper. The latter making the former an ever-greater challenge.

"Are you feeling alright, bro?" Justin looked at Declan and smiled, stifling the laugh. "You're not going to scare me that easily, dude."

Justin laughed and slapped his brother on the shoulder before walking back to the group, which were starting to move away, Declan gave a heavy sigh. He cast one last looked back at the cave entrance as they walked. He saw the mouth of the cave, and the first few stalactites that descended from the mouth like stumpy teeth, and there they were, just blindly walking down the gullet of the beast, without thinking twice.

Turning back to the group, Declan saw they had already started to descend, the path making a quick decline, and so he pushed away his reservations and hurried to catch up, almost slipping on this second step.

After the initial sharp descent and a hard-right turn, the path shallowed considerably and widened so that they could walk more as a group than a procession. Even just a few meters in, the gloom of the cave pressed in around them. Their helmets were equipped with mounted lights, and there was also lighting strategically placed along the walk, but not to the point where it detracted from the impression of the cave.

Justin and Declan were towards the rear of the cluster, along with Zeke, his wife, and Tara, who kept stopping to look back towards Justin and Declan, flashing a smile. Ahead of them, the ranger was talking about something and pointing towards the left where the cave floor was still level with them. Mounds of minerals were starting to rise, like the rolling hills that lead into a mountain range further down the road. Each reflected different colors when viewed from different angles and certainly made an impressive start to the tour.

They continued walking and the air grew damp, the odor of water heavy on the air, bringing with it a mildew-laden aftertaste with every breath. The walls were also damp and in some places coated with a thin layer of slime.

The path narrowed for the first time, and murmurs of excitement ran through the group like a shiver traveling down a man's spine passed the common over to the next cell and the next one until the whole body felt as if an ice cube and been drawn down its length.

The floor beyond the path began to drop and they were soon into the first cavern area. The lighting here was minimal until the park ranger turned on a powerful spotlight. Mounted on a tripod, it reminded Justin of the binoculars the kids had used during their trip to the Grand Canyon that summer. A couple of dollars and the machines spring to life giving them a close-up view of what would have otherwise been too far away to be of any significance.

The light cut through the gloom and lit up the floor below them. The drop was not far, but enough for the darkness to hide it from them completely.

One member of the group gasped as they saw the floor come to life, the powerful beam sending the bugs and insects that lived their lives in darkness scurrying for shelter.

"There are bugs down here?" a shocked voice rose from within the group, one of the younger members, who neither Justin or Declan had been officially introduced to.

Silence was the only answer that she received, with nobody wanting to dignify it with a response.

The ranger swept the beam over the floor, showing two particularly large stalagmites that rose from the base of the cave like the flowing humps on the back of a camel. They rose almost to the same height as the walkway they were standing on. The torch rose, illuminating the wall beyond and up to the cave ceiling where smaller formations hung down like teeth. The descending tentacles of washed-away rock and minerals had much sharper points than their rising brethren and held a much more sinister appearance as a result.

Justin watched as a large creature that looked like a centipede rushed across the wall, disappearing from the searchlight with haste. Its body moved swiftly, with a fluid-like ease, but even in the brief view he had, it made him think of the soft toys he and Declan had been ridiculing at the mall.

"Are those what I think they are?" Zeke asked, his voice booming even when kept to a whisper.

"Yep, bats. This cave is home to one of the largest bat colonies in the country. We regularly get scientists coming through to study them."

The light swept along the rows of animals, all huddled close together, their wings wrapped around them as if trying to keep warm in the cool air of the cave.

"Okay, follow me, the path splits into two up here, but because we are a small group, we will keep together. We will take a right-hand fork and walk around what we call the central column to the larger chamber and the spring," Ranger Tim instructed, and everybody listened like a congregation to its minister. "There is a deep drop as we pass the central column, and the path is fenced off as a result. Please do not lean over the fence."

It didn't take more than a minute before someone leaned over the fencing and stroked the central pillar, claiming excitedly that it was as wet as it looked. Justin shook his head and paused to stare at the giant column. Zeke and his wife stopped also, while Tara stood back against the opposite wall, clearly unenthused with the idea of getting any closer to the large drop the ranger had mentioned.

"It's quite remarkable, isn't it?" Zeke spoke, his voice filled with wonder.

Justin looked at the column, and the longer he did, the more he came to realize that Zeke was right. The column appeared to have no connection with either side of the cave, rising up above their heads where it was consumed with darkness, while continuing to plunge deeper beneath their feet, with a similar detachment to all other parts of the cave.

"Nobody knows how the column was formed, but there are many who believe it was not a purely natural process," Tim spoke, stressing all the right words to add more intrigue to his story.

"You mean like the supernatural?" the same voice that was shocked by the presence of the bugs in the cave spoke up.

"No, you dolt, he means man-made," one of the girl's friends interrupted, causing a titter of amusement to flit through the group.

"Oh," the voice answered, blissfully unaware of the sarcasm threaded through the words.

"Is there any record of mining going on in these caves?" someone asked.

"Nothing official, but the history of these caves is surrounded by a little more mystery than most. The entrance we came through was, shall we say, assisted with its development. Originally, there was only one known main entrance to the caves and that was kept on private property owned by a very wealthy family from the area. It was only after they handed the land over to the state that the true depths of the mines were discovered." The offering of a local legend with just enough enunciation to imply some sort of dark secret got the attention of the group, who turned towards the ranger eager to hear more.

"How deep does it go?" a young boy asked. He couldn't have been long into double figures and was the youngest member of the group by some way, his parents standing protectively either side of him.

"A lot deeper than we are going to go," Tim answered.

"But how deep? Have you seen the bottom, or does it go on forever?" The boy was not going to be dismissed with such an answer.

"Nothing goes on forever. I've never seen the bottom, but I know it has one." Tim shuffled on the spot, turning to lead them further before anybody else had the chance to answer questions, or before the inquisitive nature of boys on an adventure rose once more.

The path continued to descend, drawing closer to the floor, and the feeling of being underground truly impressed itself upon the group. The temperature dropped, and they could almost feel the weight of the rocks sitting around and above them. The walls were jagged and untouched, formed by nature, and as a result, they needed to be cautious with where they walked. On several occasions, the sharp sound of a helmet hitting a jutting section of the cave rang out, including Declan, whose attention had been taken by a mark on the wall that looked like a cave painting of some early sort. He didn't get a chance to study the image in any way because the group was moving through the narrow passage without pausing to enjoy where they were. Everybody was focused on reaching the next cavern rather than looking at what was immediately around them.

"You alright?" Justin asked, dropping back to help his brother readjust his helmet.

"Yeah, just wasn't paying attention. Did you see those markings back there?" Declan asked, looking back the way they had come.

"Markings?"

"I'll take that as a no," Declan said, turning his head back towards his brother. "Come and take a look at this quickly."

Declan grabbed his brother's arm and pulled him back the few meters before he had a chance to argue.

"We should keep up with the group," Justin said.

"It's right here, look." Declan focused the lamp from his helmet on the wall. The image was not as clear on a second, closer viewing than he had thought, but it was clearly a drawing of some sort; a human figure with short, squat body and a large head. It was standing over another similar figure, although the second figure lacked a lot of detail compared to the first.

"Well, the ranger said it was privately owned for a long time. It was probably some kids or something messing around," Justin said. "Besides, cave paintings are pretty common."

"I know, but doesn't it all just feel a little bit off to you?" Declan felt his skin crawl as he looked around, feeling more than just the presence of the walls closing in on him.

There was something else there too, a steady shuffling noise that was bled subtly into the general echo of the cave.

"I think this place has you spooked," Justin said, trying not to laugh. "Stay close to me, I'll keep you safe."

Declan punched his brother playfully on the arm. "Fuck you." He smiled, and they hurried on after the group. Declan smiled, but he could not shake the feeling of dread. It clung to him like a veil, clouding his senses, threatening to smother him at any moment.

They found the others gathered together on a small viewing platform. The passage had widened and the cool air felt like a welcome release to Declan's sweat-covered skin. People were taking turns to walk to the viewing platform, crouching down to peer at something on a far lower level than where they stood.

"Is that the spring?" the young boy asked.

"No, this is actually a secluded pool created within the cave. It has, to the best of my knowledge, never been touched by man. Of course, I can only speak from what I've been told, but there is no way down or back up from it." Ranger Tim was talking to the boy, playing a heavy layer of mystique onto everything, but for Declan, the world held a sinister undertone.

"This place probably holds a lot of secrets, right?" Declan spoke up before he realized.

"Oh yes, more than we could ever truly hope to understand," Tim replied, getting back to his feet and ready to lead them further.

Before they set off, Justin and Declan took the chance to jump onto the platform. Crouching down, the lights from their helmets reflected on the surface of the water in a pool that looked to have been cut and set into the rock face.

"Now that's impressive," Justin said, staring at the shimmering surface.

"It sure is," Declan replied. "It's like in its own little private space."

"Pretty cool," Justin said, nodding and turning.

The brothers walked back to the group, who were waiting for them.

"Okay, perfect, now if everybody would follow me, we have one large descent until we reach the main chamber," Tim spoke, holding his hand in the air as he did, like a child at school. "I will ask you all to please stay behind me. Don't be tempted to jump ahead, the path moves this way for a reason. There is also a bridge that we need to cross. Please do not crowd it, but also do not worry. It is as sturdy as anything you have ever come across." Declan couldn't help but wonder if that was really the case, why there was a need to mention it at all, but he decided better than to voice his question.

They continued walking, hitting a steady decline until they suddenly found themselves in a snaking maze of ropes, twisting their way back and forth in long sweeping turns, like a group of tourists standing in line for a ride at Disneyland.

The snaking passage went on for some time, and while there appeared to be no obvious reason for its design, everybody neatly followed the path laid out for them.

"Why do I get the impression that there is going to be a rollercoaster waiting for us at the end of this?" Justin asked his brother.

"Yeah, maybe some little mine cars that we all have to sit in," Declan answered and the brothers both started laughing.

"Maybe they can even put in a nice sudden drop, take us down to the goblins," Zeke added, making the brothers jump with his sudden intrusion. Neither had been aware he was that close by.

"That would be something," Declan said, laughing.

"You boys just never grow up, do you?" Zeke's wife said in mock despair. "Come on, you old goat, before you get us into trouble for falling behind."

Zeke rolled his eyes at his wife's demands and turned back to follow her.

They reached the end of the queue and were mildly disappointed when they saw there was no ride waiting for them. The cave had grown wide and shallow around them, the walls moving further away while the ceiling above their heads inched closer to them, the jagged spikes that descended shallowing to little more than an undulating surface. The effect, for those that were paying attention, was disorienting and made it feel as if they were being crushed.

As short ways ahead of them, the group could see the bridge that Tim had mentioned. It was about twenty feet long and connected to portions of a cave together, allowing their tour to continue. The bridge looked sturdy enough from distance, and Tim moved across it without hesitation.

The group followed; only the young boy paused to look over the side while his mother shuffled along, terrified of falling.

Declan and Justin were part of the last few people to cross, doing so without a second thought, until a strange howl echoed through the cave. The sound came rumbling through the cave, surrounding them, making it impossible to identify a specific direction. The noise swirled around them like an autumn wind, whipping it into a frenzy as if attacking those caught in its path.

Declan turned around, feeling the constant draft against his skin, convinced it was the rushing wind of a charging devil rising up to claim them.

In their group, someone screamed. The bridge rattled and shook. Zeke and his wife froze, holding on to both sides of the structure as if they could somehow hold it aloft.

"Everybody, head this way, toward me," Ranger Tim's voice called out, trying to stem the rising panic. "Nothing to be alarmed about."

His words were drowned out the din of crumbling rock, swiftly followed by the unmistakable sound of wrenched metal. It echoed through the chamber, telling everybody exactly what was happening, but not giving them the time needed to react. Declan looked around and felt his brother's hands clamp onto him, the grip one fueled by terror. A heartbeat later and the ground beneath his feet shifted. The bridge collapsed, dropping several feet before stopping with a sudden lurch.

The nature of the stop sent everybody on the bridge stumbling, and before them, Zeke lost his balance. He cried out in pain, and Declan saw the way the man's ankle buckled beneath him.

"Give me your hand," Tim called out, reaching down towards them.

Tara was closest, scrambling against the wall. She jumped and took hold of Tim's outstretched arm, but it was too late. The bridge gave out and suddenly, they were all falling.

Justin screamed.

Zeke screamed.

Tilly, Zeke's wife, screamed, and Declan knew for sure that he screamed.

They fell into the darkness, swallowed by the cave. Looking back, the crowd of panicked faces watched on helpless. Tara still swung from Ranger Tim's hand, her legs kicking frantically in the air as she fought more than helped her escape.

Darkness consumed them, the lights of their helmets trying in vain to fight against the totality of the cave, thrashing around not settling long enough to show anything. It was cold and the rushing air was a shrill whistle in their ears. There was no way of knowing when it would be over, not until the jarring impact, and the explosion of pain that overtook them.

CHAPTER ELEVEN

Justin thought he was a dead man. He first realized it as they started to fall. The sudden stop and the pain merely confirmed it for him.

The acoustics of the cave did not help, amplifying the sound and throwing it around so that echoes and fresh cries of pain mixed together into an indistinguishable noise. A sweeping, surging tide of icy cold enveloped him, sucking him down further.

Water.

It rushed into his mouth, flooding his lungs before Justin could react. He fought, unable to separate the feeling of pain from anything else. All he knew was that he would not die without a fight. Justin swam, kicking and pulling himself, unsure if he was even swimming in the right direction.

His lungs burned and he could feel that something wasn't quite right in his body. His left arm was not working properly. His movements grew labored, his body tired, and just as Justin was considering admitting defeat, he broke the surface of the pool. The noise that greeted him was the cries of the others that had fallen. He could hear them splashing around in the water but had no idea where they were.

The darkness was completed. Justin couldn't tell if he was a few feet from solid ground, or if there was no form of sanctuary to be found.

The water was moving. He could feel the current pulling him. Faster and faster, they were descending, dropping even deeper into the earth. At least that was how it felt.

The rock came out of nowhere, a solid, immovable object that caught Justin's body and sent a fresh wave of pain shooting through him.

The rock was cold and slick with slime. There was nowhere for Justin to find purchase, while the growing power of the current pulled at his legs, trying to drag him down. Panic began to creep in, the sound of the water roaring in his ears.

The blow was sudden, and there was no way to see what hit him. He thought he felt a hand grab at him, but he was too bust struggling and fighting to stay alive. The pull of the water was too much, and he sank below the surface, sucked down by the greedy water gods. Rocks scraped and stabbed at him, etching burning abrasions into his flesh. The underground tunnel acted like a water slide of death, trapping whoever it caught until they drowned.

Justin was tired and weak; the cold water had numbed his body, but then suddenly, he was falling again, crashing down into a second pool, the water even colder than the first. It was shallower, however, and Justin could push himself from the bottom back up to the surface.

The light came from nowhere, blinding him. It filled Justin's field of vision, thrusting him from blindness into blindness, albeit from the opposite side of the spectrum.

Someone grabbed him by the arm and hauled him out of the water. The ground was hard and jagged beneath him, but Justin lay there, exhausted, allowing the pain to settle so he could get an idea of what had happened. Everything still felt like a blur.

"Your shoulder is out of the socket," Declan's familiar voice rang in his ear. It wavered in and out of range, but Justin would never not be able to recognize his brother.

"Dec?" Justin couldn't muster the strength to add anything else to the statement.

"Hold on. This is going to hurt." Justin felt Declan's hands slide under him, elevating his shoulder.

He felt a sharp pain shoot this his left arm as his brother tried to move it into position. There was a sudden burst of pressure, and the pain increased to a level Justin had not previously known. The audible pop rang in his ears and made him think of a bone snapping. Then suddenly, the worst of the pain was gone, dropping down to a dull ache.

"There you go," Declan said. "Wait here. I need to look for the others."

He was gone again, and Justin was left in the dark. His heart thumped in his ears, and he could still hear the splashes of the others in the water.

It hurt, but Justin pushed himself into a sitting position, Justin could make out Declan in the dark, the light from his helmet tracing over the water like a searchlight. The splashes had died down, replaced by the sound of someone weeping. It came from close by.

"Hello?" Justin called.

The crying stopped for a moment, the creator of the sound startled by his voice.

"Who's there?" a frail voice asked, sounding on the verge of breaking.

"It's Justin. I was on the bridge ... when it fell." It was a woman, Justin could tell that much, but his brain was still scrambled; he couldn't think clearly enough to place anybody else on the bridge at the moment of its collapse.

"Who are you?" he asked, unashamed.

"Tilly," the voice came back, even softer.

"Zeke's wife," Justin said, not so much a question but more a statement.

"Yes. Where are we?"

"I don't know," Justin answered, trying to pinpoint her position to him.

"Have you seen Zeke?" Her voice was almost gone, the question too hard for her to pose.

"I can't see anything," Justin said, his words making Tilly cry once more.

Justin couldn't think of anything else to say, so he surrendered to the darkness and the pain. His shoulder ached, his head throbbed, and he could feel the warmth of blood trickling down his neck. His body stung, like hitting a belly flop into the pool, And then there was the all-encompassing pain that hid specific injuries under the cloud of general agony. Being blind didn't help, and had it not been for the glint of the wet rock under the beam of Declan's helmet light, he would have been terrified that the blindness was the result of injury rather than location.

He tried to move each limb in turn and assess for injury, but his head was too fuzzy to tell him anything.

"Justin, dude, you still with me?" Declan was back, his light shining right on Justin's face.

Justin winced, squinting as the pain in his head increased sharply. "Yeah, but dude, the light."

"Oh, sorry." The light disappeared for a moment and came back from the side, set against the rock in such a way that the light direct glow of the bulb hit the wet rock, and its reflection cast a dim glow over an area of the cavern they had landed in.

"Where are we?" Justin asked, his head swimming.

Declan crouched down beside his brother and lifted his head, peering closely at him. "I have no idea. Best I can tell is we landed in an underground river and it pulled us down deeper into the caves." Declan spoke, but the words were merely an answer to a question. His attention was focused on his brother's head.

"How bad is it?" Justin winced, dizziness washing over him every time Declan moved his head.

"It's an ugly gash, but you will live. We can bandage it up and hopefully slow the bleeding," Declan said, grabbing a couple of lengths of cloth and wrapping it around his brother's head.

"Where did you get that from?" Justin needed to talk, to fight off crippling nausea that churned his stomach and the encroaching waves of tempting darkness.

"I got it from Tara, it's a piece of her shirt," Declan said, but from the tone of his voice, Justin was sure that there was something else that his brother wasn't saying.

Carefully, Declan bandaged Justin's head, packing the wound as best he could with the second piece of fabric, which he rolled into a ball.

"There, I'm no miracle worker, and it will probably leave you with a nasty scar, but it's the best I can do." Declan helped his brother up to his feet. "We need to keep moving, and well, I need your help with all this, bro."

"What?" Justin asked, woozy, leaning on Declan with close to his whole body weight. He felt increasing waves of nausea hit him in the gut, wrenching it as if someone were throwing his insides through a wood chipper.

Declan led Justin through the dark. They passed Tilly, who was curled up in a ball, her back pressed against the side of the rock. He had been drawn to the light Declan created, like a moth, and when they looked at her, she shook her head wildly, her eyes wide with terror.

The sound of falling water grew in intensity, and Justin realized that they were moving closer to the water.

"Wait here," Declan said, the support for his brother disappearing as Declan dropped to the cave floor.

Justin swayed on his feet as thundering gusts of pain shot through him, lighting up the darkness of his mind like flashes of fork lightning during a heavy summer storm.

Declan rose again, and soon another shaft of light appeared, slicing through the darkness as best it could manage.

"Here, take this." Declan handed the helmet to Justin, who took it and placed it on his head.

"Is this what you wanted to show me?" Justin asked, confused.

"No, she's over there," Declan answered, his hand appearing in the beam of light, pointing further ahead.

Justin moved forward, peering into the darkness when suddenly, Tara appeared. Only, she no longer looked like the pretty young woman that she had been when they met a few hours earlier.

Now, her face was swollen and purple, her skull split open with thick globs of grey brain tissue bubbling up from the gash that had been created. Her neck was twisted so that her head lay at an angle that did not work with the position of her body. Likewise, her legs tucked up beneath her, while one of her arms was snapped, the bone piercing her skin and rising into the air, its jagged tip clinging to strips of meat that it had pulled along with it.

"Jesus, what happened?" Justin asked, covering his hand with his mouth.

"Best I can guess is she fell and hit hard, and then when we came through and into the pool, she got thrown too far and hit the ground," Declan said. "What are we going to do with her?"

Justin thought about it for a second before his response came. "We have to leave her here." He felt bad for reaching such a conclusion so fast, but the truth was staring him in the face. They couldn't carry her with them. They needed to get out.

"I was hoping you would say that," Declan said. "Because I didn't want to think that I was a cold-hearted bastard."

Justin gave his brother a pat on the back.

"Was there anybody else?" Justin asked.

"I don't know. I found her, then I found you. Tilly pulled herself out of the water, best I can tell. She's a tough one."

"Seems like it. What about Zeke? He was on the bridge with us too." Justin's head pulsed in time with the pounding beats of his heart, but he felt good for being up and about, or as good as he could expect to feel given their current situation.

"Shit, I wasn't thinking. Let's have a look around for him." Declan took his brother's arm, and together they made their way over the cave floor.

The water's edge was slippery, the rocks covered in slimy algae, and it was far from a smooth walking surface.

They didn't need to walk long before they found Zeke. His large frame was hard to miss, even as he lay half-submerged in the water.

"Zeke, Zeke, buddy, can you hear me?" Declan dropped to his knees, while Justin remained standing, casting light onto the scene.

The large man's face was covered in blood, his large beard caked in it. He was breathing, his large, barrel chest rising and falling with jagged, irregular breaths.

"We need to get him out of the water." Declan moved and took hold of the man under both arms.

The moment he started to pull, Zeke's eyes open and a gush of blood burst from his mouth like a geyser. He gagged and choked, his eyes filling with panic as the light blinded him. He tried to move and thrash, but he lacked the energy, and Declan was easily able to calm him.

"Easy, buddy, easy, Zeke." Declan crouched even lower, so his face would come into view.

Zeke mumbled something, unable to speak on account of the blood that was filling his mouth.

"That's not good," Justin said, watching as the man made another gargled attempt to talk, which resulted in more blood being vomited onto his face.

"Take a look for any injuries. I can't move it, and I don't think it's just his weight." Declan strained as he spoke, once again trying to move the man from the water.

Moving around them, Justin kept the light focused on the pair, and as a result, almost tripped over a large rock that was blocking his path. Catching himself at the last minute, he cursed as a lightning bolt of pain streaked across this mind's eye, blinding him temporarily.

When everything came back into focus, he was where he needed to be and crouched down best Zeke. That man's breath had increased, each exhalation coming with a grunt of pain. It didn't take long for Justin to see the problem. A large shard of rock was stuck in the man's back, and their attempts to move him only served to drive it deeper.

"Bro, stop, stop now," Justin spat, the words rolling over each other in his urgency to get them spoken.

"What?" Declan asked.

"I think he's got a broken spine. We can't move him." The words were not lost on Zeke who made a terrified whimpering sound and turned his head to look at Justin. His eyes were wide with fear, and the blood-spattered face only served to make him look even more feral.

Declan laid Zeke's head on the ground and moved beside his brother. He saw the large rock shard piercing the man's spine and the flow of blood collecting in a pool at its base.

"Fuck," Declan whispered, his words drowned out by the sound of the cascading water. "What do we do?"

"We have to find a way out and get help," Justin said.

Declan couldn't stop staring at the Zeke. "What about him? I don't think he will survive if we leave him here. The water is freezing. He'll get hypothermia or something."

"If we move him, we will do more damage than good," Justin pointed out.

"Better paralyzed than dead," Declan offered as a response. "What if we take that rock out, and at least bring him up to Tilly."

Justin was quiet for a moment, thinking things through. "Alright, we do it quick. You roll and I'll pull it free."

Zeke was watching them both intently, his eyes bright and focused on them. While he could not have heard their conversation, it was clear that he understood what they were planning. With his face set, he watched as Declan moved into position and managed to give a nod.

"One, two ..." Declan rolled Zeke to his left.

"Three," Justin grabbed the shard of rock and yanked it free.

The bellow that escaped Zeke's lungs echoed around the cavern and seemed to grow loud rather than fade away.

"It's bleeding a lot. Shit," Justin said, panicked. "But ... but I don't think it was in his spine. It was off to one side."

"Here, use this." Declan's words were followed by a ripping sound. A wad of cloth was thrust into Justin's hands, and he used it to pad the wound, pushing as hard as he could to stop the flow of blood.

"Give me his belt," Justin said, as he fought the need to pass out.

"What?"

"His belt, give it to me, I need something to hold the bandage in place," Justin said, as his arms grew tired.

Declan made quick work of undoing Zeke's belt, pulling it free. The large leather strap was just long enough to wrap around the man's body, the wound being just higher than the bulk of his belly. With it pulled tight and fastened, Justin could release the pressure and drop to the ground.

"Thank ... thank you," Zeke coughed out.

His breathing was still heavy, but it seemed more stable than before.

"We need to get you out of the water. It's not far. Can you move your legs?" Declan asked.

"I think so," Zeke spoke slowly, his words slurred through the pain.

With a grunt, the big man managed to raise his knee and put his foot flat on the floor. He growled in pain but pushed on. Grabbing Declan's offered hand, he twisted his body and rolled onto his knees.

It took a little while, but between the three of them, they managed to get Zeke up to a vertical base. He sways on his feet, unsteady, like a tired boxer going into the twelfth round, with nothing left to fight for but his pride.

"I'm good. I'm good," Zeke said after they stumbled part of the way. "Just keep that light shining straight."

"You sure?" Declan asked, wary of letting the man go.

"Boy, I'm tougher than a tanned hide. I've been through worse stuff than this and come out swinging the other side." A surge of strength ran through Zeke as he brushed off the brother's helpful hands and set off under his own steam.

Justin looked at Declan, and in the light of their head torch, he saw his brother looking right back at him. Neither had anything to say at that moment which would accurately capture the man.

"Tilly, Tilly, are you alright?" Zeke called out the moment he saw his wife curled up against the wall. Her face was pale and gaunt, her eyes gazing into the darkness as if blind, incapable of making out anything, so focused on nothing.

"Zeke?" the older woman spoke as if coming out of a trance, following the voice of her beloved as it helped her fight back from the depths to which she had sunk.

"That's right, honey. I'm here." Zeke reached for his wife, and against all degrees of logic, he was able to help her to her feet. His back was soaked with a mixture of blood and sweat, but it was clear that he was not going to let anything slow him down.

While the couple embraced, Declan and Justin turned the lights of their helmets away from the water and to the walls of the cavern. They had no idea where they were, but it was pretty evident that they could not go back the way they had come.

A quick look gave them four different tunnels that they could take, each one varying sizes, but all large enough for them to walk through. The entrances were spherical and had a strangely manmade look to them.

"Something made these tunnels," Justin said as they stood against the opening of the one closest to them. "The finish isn't machine smooth, but there is no way these happened here by accident."

"That's good then. If someone made it this far and carved these tunnels, then they must be a way out somewhere back there," Zeke offered. He was sweating profusely and looked far paler than he had earlier in the day.

"Maybe," Declan answered.

"Maybe?" Justin looked at his brother. "Bro, Zeke's got a point."

"He does, I'm just saying we don't know what is down here, or where these things lead. We just need to be careful, that's all," Declan stammered, unable to put into words the strange feeling that was tickling the back of his mind.

"Let's take a moment, decide which tunnel we are going to go down, and make an order to it," Zeke said, getting as close as he could come to saying he needed to stop for a moment. He wiped a meaty hand across his forehead.

They studied the tunnels and agreed that everything they knew totaled up to nothing, and so they took the first tunnel. Declan went first, as he had a working helmet and the least injuries. Zeke and Tilly moved together behind him, while Justin brought up the rear. He also wore a helmet, which meant the group created enough light for them all to see by as they picked their way through the tunnel. They spoke very little at first, the silence of the cave an overbearing weight on their spirits.

The conversation started between husband and wife, talking about their plans once they got back home. It was a stilted conversation, that lacked a great deal of conviction, but it was enough to get the spirits of the group up a little.

"I'm taking those tikes to the store and buying them whatever toys they want. I'm spoiling them rotten every chance I get," Zeke said, his voice sounding more powerful now that he was up and moving. "What about you boys? You got any family waiting for you out there?"

"I've got a wife and three daughters," Justin answered.

"I bet you're going to spoil them rotten too, ain't you?" Zeke didn't turn around as he spoke, but he didn't need to for Justin to know he was talking to him.

"For sure. We had a holiday planned already but hell, I think I'm just going to spend the rest of my life on holiday, traveling the world." Justin allowed himself to be swept away by the image, which gave his spirits a buoyancy that they had lacked.

"What about you, Declan?" Tilly asked, her voice timid and small.

"No, I don't have a family yet," Declan answered quickly. "I plan on starting one though."

"That's good. A man your age, in his prime, a family is what keeps you going." Tilly addressed nobody in particular, her voice trailing off as she lost herself in her thoughts.

"I just need to find a good woman that's willing to take me. I've got a bit of a past that many will find off-putting," Declan said as he stopped walking, sweeping the torch around, even though there was only one way to keep moving and that was straight ahead.

"If you find the right woman, she will love you no matter what, and you will love her the same way," Zeke added, the big man showing his sappy side as he put his arm around Tilly and squeezed.

"I hope so, I've got some baggage that takes a lot of forgiving," Declan answered, but it was clear, especially to Justin, that his brother was really talking to himself.

"You will be surprised what love can do to a person. Besides, nothing can be so bad that people will run away before getting to know you," Zeke said, the only one of the group that seemed oblivious to Declan's voice internal monologue.

"Being the guy that murdered his father is not often a subject that goes down too well with the ladies. Not the sort I want to be around, anyway," Declan answered before realizing what he had said.

Justin cringed, unsure what to expect from the older couple between them after hearing such a revelation.

They were indeed quiet for a few moments but kept walking at the same pace. "Your father, well, that's definitely a hard one to bring up in conversation. Did you have a good reason?" Zeke asked, his voice calm and thoughtful.

"He abused Justin and me for eighteen years, and one day, I just had enough," Declan answered quickly and easily. Justin wondered how often he had sat and spoken with anybody about things that had happened.

Justin knew how much he had spent on therapists and specialists in order to conquer his demons. He had never thought about how his brother had coped with everything, a realisation that carried a great amount of guilt with it.

"Then it sounds to me like it is not as cold-hearted as you make it sound, son." Zeke's voice changed, and his paternal side kicked in. "A parent should love their child unconditionally, and how any could hurt their own flesh and blood, in any way, is beyond me." Zeke stopped talking a split second before Declan brought them to a stop again.

There was no need to ask why. They all heard it.

Footsteps.

CHAPTER TWELVE

"What was that?" Tilly asked, spinning around to peer into the darkness.

Both Declan and Justin also turned, their lights looking back the way they had come. They saw nothing, heard nothing but the thundering of their own hearts. Yet, they all knew what they had heard.

"We're not alone," Declan said.

"Maybe it's a rescue party or another tour group," Tilly's hopeful voice spoke up.

None of them believed it. The sounds they had heard were sharp and too soft and fast for human feet.

"Justin, keep an eye out behind us. I'll keep eyes front. We need to keep moving, but stay alert, something is down here." Declan took charge, a role he fell into comfortably. It was one that suited him, and once again showed Justin just how much his brother could have accomplished.

"Tilly?" Zeke called as they started to move.

A scream shattered the silence of the cave, conveying a pain that no words could accurately describe.

"Tilly!" Zeke roared, and both beams of helmet light crisscrossed one another as the brothers frantically sought to find Tilly.

They found her sitting on the floor of the cave, her face pale and dripping with sweat as if she had just walked out of a spinning class.

"Oh God, Tilly, are you alright?" Zeke moved to his wife, followed by the brothers.

"Here, we need to keep moving," Declan said, offering Tilly a hand.

She reached up, slowly, her hands trembling, silent tears streaming from her eyes, their silvery trail cutting a path through the grime, exposing the flesh beneath and serving to make her face even more agonized.

Declan took her and helped her to her feet.

"Oh shit," Justin said as he stared at Tilly's belly. The fabric of her shirt had been ripped open, and two puncture wounds were visible, the red stain spreading through the surrounding material.

95

"What did that?" Zeke asked, reaching for his wife, the strain on his face evident as he took her into his arms.

"There." Justin pointed with his helmet and the light reflected on a long fissure in the rock face. "I saw something."

As they watched, a pair of bright yellow eyes appeared, reflecting the light of the torch back at them.

The group jumped, and while none would admit it individually, they all screamed. Tilly groaned, growing limp in Zeke's arms.

"Tilly!" he cried out.

Declan turned to look at Tilly, while Justin froze on the fissure. The eyes had gone, but he could hear something moving, and he could see movement, black within the black.

"We need to move, now," Justin said, as the first long, jointed legs appeared, emerging through the small opening like the tentacles of an octopus, forcing its way through an opening far too small for its body to logically fit through.

More legs appeared, and suddenly the bulbous, hairy body followed. The legs dug into the rock as they heaved the body free. Three sets of yellow eyes stared at the group, boring into them, as the rest of the body appeared.

The cave birthed the creature, which scrambled and scratched at the rock, trying desperately to pull itself through.

It looked like a spider, with the number of legs and the general shape of its emerging body. The only problem being, it was as large as a medium-sized dog.

"Jay, I need some help here," Declan called, snapping Justin out of his freeze.

Justin turned and saw Zeke and Declan holding Tilly, her legs long and limp behind her. Her shirt had ridden up in their unorthodox grip, and Justin could not only see two similar puncture marks on her spine but the blackening tissue around it.

"We need to move," Justin called, jumping to take over from Zeke, who had picked a bad time to start succumbing to his injuries.

As Justin lifted Tilly's arm to place it around his shoulder, he heard a wet squelching sound. Tilly threw her head back and screamed as if she were howling at the moon.

"Hurry," Justin urged, certain that the noise he had heard was the creature finally freeing itself from the cave wall.

The brothers quickened their pace, and with a final scream, Tilly grew still and inexplicably lighter in their arms.

"Something's wrong," Declan said. "Holy fucking balls of shit."

His cry startled Justin and both men jumped back, inadvertently dropping Tilly's upper body to the ground. Her lower half lay a few meters behind them, ripped apart around the middle, in line with the points of the spider bite.

In the panicked light of their helmets, the blood and trail of organs took on an even more disturbing lilt.

"Tilly!" Zeke bellowed, running back towards his wife's legs. His foot slipped in the slick pool of blood and he fell into a heap, his wife's insides coating him as he rolled, tangling himself in a never-ending string of bloated, blue intestines.

Justin moved quickly, grabbing Zeke and heaving on his large frame, pulling him through the puddle of gore, just as the dog-sized spider creature reached Tilly's legs. The creature gave a strange hissing sound before rearing up on its hind set of legs. Large fangs unfurled from beneath the creature's head. As thick as a man's wrist at their base, they twitched and grew even longer as twin fleshy appendages, as thin as straws and tapered to a fine point, descended. Striking fast, the creature speared Tilly's legs, sinking fang deep into the soft, blood-smeared flesh. They could see the fangs pulse and twitch as a hungry sucking sound rang out. They saw the severed limbs bloat momentarily, as whatever toxin the creature released flooded them. The creature soon drank down the rotting flesh to nothing more than the skin sack and bone. The toxin rotted the limb in an instant, as evident by the stream of black necrotic flesh than leaked from Tilly's severed waist.

"What the fuck is that?" Declan asked, frozen as he stared helplessly as the thing drank Tilly dry.

"I have no idea, but we need to get moving," Justin growled back to his brother. "Give me a hand."

The two men worked to free Zeke from his wife's intestines. The man was in shock, his entire body shaking as his brain tried to process what had happened.

Their hands slipped on the gore-covered entrails, but they managed to find their grip and free Zeke's legs. Hauling him to his feet, they pushed and pulled him along, moving at a run, charging deeper into the tunnel, not stopping to look if they were being followed

As they moved, the tunnel started to narrow around them, tightening quickly until they were no longer able to stand fully upright. This was a big problem for Zeke, who frame was exceedingly large in all dimensions.

"Is that thing still after us?" Declan panted from the front of the line.

"I have no idea," Justin answered, barely able to catch his breath.

Against their better judgment, the trio slowed down, the broken shell that was Zeke panting and sobbing in equal measure.

"I don't see anything," Justin said, taking a moment to lean forward, resting his weight on his knees. His head pounded, and the longer he stood still, the more he felt his muscles turn to jelly beneath him.

"Til ... my sweet woman." Zeke crashed to the floor, his body shaking, the metallic odor of blood heavy in the air around him. "I don't understand. That thing ... it was an alien or something, it had to be."

From his position on the cave ground, Zeke looked up at the two brothers, and he no longer looked like the large, happy-go-lucky-man they had first met above ground. He looked like an old man, lost and scared in a world he no longer recognized.

"We need to keep moving. There could be more of them," Declan said, adjusting the light on his helmet to give him a wider, albeit, softer beam.

Justin took it as his cue to look around the cave. His keen eyes caught scratch marks and indentations gouged into the rock, and he shuddered at the thought of what may have created them.

"What if there are more of them ahead?" Zeke asked, sounding defeated.

"Well, we know there is at least one back there, and no way out. The way I figure it, moving forward is our only option," Declan said, his honesty and simple, straightforward logic leaving them with no real room for argument.

As the tunnel got smaller, the temperature increased, and with no real movement within the air, all three men found it hard going, slowing even further when the tunnel forced them to their knees. Crawling through the dark like infants, they pushed on, stopping only when one of them heard something. From the sound of their own movements reverberating around them, to what sounded like the distant beating of a drum, the darkness amplified everything and turned it into a threat.

"It's getting mighty tight in here," Zeke growled as he shuffled forward on his belly, squirming his way through the deep caverns like a giant worm, burrowing deeper and deeper.

"Keep going, I can see something ahead," Declan called back to the guys.

The tunnel closed around them, squeezing them together. All three men sank to their bellies and managed to crawl further along through the tunnel, with Declan still in the lead, followed by Justin who had moved ahead of Zeke after their stop for a rest. It had been Zeke's insistence that he assume the rear guard position, simply because he was the weak link in their chain.

"Stop here a second," Declan spoke, passing the message to his brother.

Declan inched further forward, his head and shoulders found a wide-open space. The chamber was a large affair with thick stone pillars rising out of the ground and stretching up to the ceiling high above their heads. He was close, and wormed his way further through the opening until suddenly, he was free, and dropped down to the hard ground beneath them.

Declan pushed himself to his feet, his shoulders giving a loud crack as he straightened. It felt great being able to stand, while the cool air of the cavern was a welcome change to the stifling heat of the tight passageway.

"Justin?" Declan called. "Come on through, there's another cavern."

The words echoed around the space, which Declan had yet to get a scope of in terms of its size. Looking up, the helmet light reflected on the mineral deposits in the rock and twinkled like the night sky. Turning around, he saw the tips of several stalactites that emerged from the dark like incisors, locked and loaded, ready to clamp down at any moment.

Justin emerged through what was essentially a large crack in the wall rather than any official tunnel and dropped to the ground. Declan caught him and stood with him for a moment. Both men panting, their bodies aching and their muscles exhausted.

"Guys, um ... a little help here," Zeke spoke, as he balanced halfway through the opening.

At first glance, Justin's mind was immediately brought back to watching the spider escape the wall. Shaking his head, he drove that memory away, locking it down into the box of long-forgotten secrets and pains, where it would never need to be looked at again.

Zeke was stuck, wedged fast in the rock. They tugged and pulled on him, but he barely moved. The man struggled, his chest being crushed, unable to take real breaths, but even with his strength fueled by adrenaline, Zeke could not to more than drag himself an inch through the wall, effectively making his predicament even worse.

"Okay, wait for a second, wait a second, there's got to be something we can do," Declan spoke, panting.

"I can't really breathe," Zeke groaned, his face turning a deep shade of red.

"It's okay, stay calm, we'll get you down," Justin said.

"Hurry, I can feel something crawling on my leg." Zeke's eyes went wide with panic, and he started to thrash around, as the realization of his words filtered through his brain. "There's something on my leg! Get it off! Get it off!"

"Calm down, hey, it will only get worse." Declan tried to calm the big man, but Zeke's thrashes turned into screams, the veins in his neck and across his forehead rising up from his body as the full extent of the agony he felt surged through him.

"Help me," Zeke spat. "It hurts, oh God, it hurts."

"We just have to pull him," Declan said, grabbing hold of one arm.

"Are you sure?" Justin looked at his brother.

"It's biting me, it's biting me. I don't want to die. I'm not ready," Zeke pleaded with Declan and Justin, his eyes wide with a childlike horror, a collection of tears, snot, and saliva dribbling from his face.

The brothers each grabbed a hand and pulled. They strained and grunted, and at one point, Justin saw nothing but a patchwork of exploding colors as pain exploded in his head. Yet somehow, they managed to move Zeke's frame. He slid through the crack, screaming like a wounded pig. When he fell to the floor, they could see why.

His lower left leg had been ravaged by something. The material of his trousers and the flesh beneath had been torn open down to the bone. Jagged strips of flesh dangled over the edges of what remained of his calf like strips of old wallpaper, still clinging on to their former glory.

"What the hell?" Declan jumped back as if the spreading pool of blood carried some hitherto unknown infection.

"Where the heck are we? What sort of place has bugs that eat people?" Justin asked, his eyes flitting from the torn-up limb to the hole in the wall they had emerged through.

"Help me," Zeke begged from the floor, as for the second time the brothers watch blood pump from his large frame.

"Here, take this," Justin said, pulling off his sweater, moving down to just the T-shirt beneath.

Handing the sweater to Declan, he watched as his brother bent down and got to work. He pressed down hard onto the injury, the squelching sound of the blood only drowned out by the rising cry in Zeke's throat. Working quickly, Justin tied off the sweater by wrapping the arms in opposing direction around the limb.

"It's as good as I can do, but we need to get him out of here," Declan said, not even trying to hide his voice for the sake of the patient.

"Then we move," Justin answered. "Let's get him up."

Together, they hauled Zeke to his feet, and somehow, his giant frame still found the strength to support himself, hopping along, he relied on the brothers for support, but refused to give up completely. The gloom of the cave seemed to lessen, and they found themselves able to pick out shapes and forms in the darkness. The crystals and minerals on the rock surface had a phosphorous quality emitting a low-wattage light which, to the trio, seemed as glorious as watching the sun rising bringing light to their world and fighting back the gloom.

The cavern was a large open place with large stalagmites rising from the ground like pillars, stretching and out of sight, the ceiling above their heads engulfed in darkness. The enormity of the space beggared belief and made them wonder how deep under the ground they had fallen.

"We should rest," Justin said.

"I don't know. I think we should keep moving. Being down here creeps me the fuck out," Declan answered, looking around distrusting, as if the shadows were conspiring to hide some new monster from them.

"Me too, but my head is spinning and I don't feel great," Justin said, "and I don't think Zeke can go much longer."

Looking at the man, his head hung low and his breaths were wet and shallow, his lungs sounding as if they were filled with fluid rather than air. Sweat fell from his face like rain, and a near sickly aroma wafted from his body.

"Okay, let's lay him down, but you need to keep moving. Head wounds are nasty." Declan had accepted the leadership role without question. "You and I can take a look around, see what options we have for getting out of this damned place."

Declan walked with a pronounced limp, something Justin only then noticed, given that they had been crawling and dragging themselves over the floor for so long.

"You're hurt," Justin said.

"Not as bad as you guys. I've had worse knocks before." Declan didn't even turn around as he moved behind one of the large pillars.

Temporarily, Declan disappeared from view, the only thing confirming his presence was the dull glow emitted from his helmet.

"You mean in prison?" Justin hesitated, not wanting to bring up the subject.

"Yeah. It wasn't always fun and games." Declan reappeared, his eyes set on Justin.

"I ... I had no idea." Justin lowered his gaze. "You never said."

"What was there to say? Hey, bro, I got my ass kicked last night because my new cellmate decided he didn't like me. Or maybe the time I got my head busted open because Mick Nare wanted to use the weight rack and I hadn't finished my set." Declan froze, realizing what he had said and more importantly, what he didn't have to say.

The brothers stopped walking, and stood a few meters apart, staring at one another. Yet, for what it was worth, they could have been on different continents in that moment in time. The gulf between them, their lives and their futures, was vast.

From behind them, in the dark, they heard Zeke groan. Walking back to him, the silence growing into something uncomfortable between them, each brother stuck to their side of the pillars.

Justin looked up, opening his mouth to speak to his brother when Declan disappeared behind the final pillar. Stopping, Justin paused waiting for his brother to reappear so that he could finally say something and break the awkwardness. Only, Declan did not re-emerge from behind the pillar. The light from his helmet still illuminated the darkness, but Declan himself had stopped.

"Bro?" Justin asked, cutting back, moving behind the stone to find his brother.

Declan was right there, standing frozen in place, his eyes staring at the pillar.

"Shhhh," he said sharply, not wanting to make a sound.

Justin looked, trying to follow his brother's line of sight. At first, he saw nothing, but he could hear it, whatever it was that had Declan so spooked; a gentle thrum, like someone drumming their fingers on a desk. Peering into the darkness, raising his head to extend the area of light, he saw it.

The creature was as thick as his arm, if not larger, and at least a meter long, but its body disappeared into the darkness and Justin had no desire to raise his head anymore if it meant revealing the rest of the creature.

"It looks like a millipede or something like that," Justin whispered, watching as the creature stopped moving, the myriad legs that protruded from its body folding inwards like hinges, bringing the creature down onto the rock.

"Can you hear that?" Declan looked at his brother, his eyes wide.

"Hear what?" Justin asked, but received the answer immediately. The sound of clacking hadn't stopped, and not just because this one creature had paused for a rest.

"There's more of them." Justin spoke the words slowly, fear stabbing into him with each one uttered.

Looking around, their light extended to cast a gloomy haze over the next pillar, where two of the same creatures were almost at ground level, their bodies over a meter long, closer to a meter and a half. Their shells were black and brown respectively, and shimmered, even in the dull light. Unlike the one on the pillar near them, these two showed no signs of taking a rest, and as soon as first legs hit the floor, they scurried away, bodies bending at a near ninety-degree angle, as the remaining portions left the pillars and hit the flat ground.

Two long antennae extended from the front of their bodies, and while there was no discernable head or eyes, there was no mistaking the crab-like pincers that extended the minute their antennae started to twitch.

"Move. Get back to Zeke," Declan said, turning just as the creature nearest them began to move, not descending the pillar, but rather, it started to swell, certain sections of its body bloating and pulsating.

"What the hell?" Declan asked, but his curiosity was not strong enough to hold him in one place.

They could see Zeke, his body flat on the floor, his barrel chest rising and falling in jagged movements.

Behind them came a shriek and the frenzied sound of hundreds of pairs of legs running. Casting a glance over his shoulder, Declan saw something that brought him to an immediate stop.

The creatures were not chasing after them, but fleeing an attack from things else.

The brown millipede was pinned beneath the bodies of two spider-like creatures that were each as large as a big house cat.

"Holy shit," Declan said, "would you look at those things."

"They're the same as those toys we saw, only bigger." Justin couldn't believe his eyes as the brown-bodied beasts tore the brown millipede apart, their long front pincers opening up to extend the length of their body before them, slicing into the creature's flesh like small saws before folding inwards, shoveling the torn-off chunks of meat into their mouths.

"Oh shit, that's not good," Declan said, backing up as another, even larger, cave spider dropped from the darkness, landing on top of the black millipede.

The creature bucked and twisted its body like a wild bronco but couldn't shake the thing loose. A thick black stinger extended from the rear of the body, rising like a reversed scorpion's tail. Striking with a lightning quickness, it skewered the millipede, which let out a sound akin to a piglet's squeal.

"Run," Justin said, not wanting to stick around to see what was going to come as a result of the attack. Turning, he came face to face with the swollen body of the first millipede, which still clung to the pillar, even though its body was bloated to three times the size. Its skin was tearing open, and each pulse of its body made the tears widen. Clear liquid spilled out, while in places where the skin was thinnest, he could see shapes moving beneath the surface.

Justin's brain willed him to move, but his feet remained soldered to the ground, fused as if the rock had pulled him down into it, holding him captive.

Justin felt Declan grab him, his hand squeezing his shoulder and yanking him backward. For a moment, it still felt as though his feet were stuck, but at the last moment, he took a stumbling step backward, and everything that held him still was broken. He stumbled, turning just as the body of the millipede burst open with a wet splat, sending a shower of pus-like goop and chunks of black exoskeleton through the cave.

That was when they came; an army of tiny cave spiders, each one a pasty, yellow color, their bodies wet and soft still. They fell from the hollowed-out carcass, tumbling to the floor, hundreds of them immediately beginning to scurry away, heading towards food.

"Run, goddammit," Declan roared, heaving his brother backward.

With the lights of their helmets bouncing around as they ran, all hell broke loose. The brothers tried to keep pace with one another, but it was impossible. The floor of the cave was littered with the rocks and jagged shards that that stabbed at them, pulling all of their attention onto their own passage. They could hear the sound of wet, scurrying bodies behind them, advancing like a wave of destruction, eager to claim them as victim number one.

Justin chanced a look over his shoulder, the light of his torch reflecting off the bodies that gave chase. They were gaining on him.

Justin turned and tripped as his feet hit something large and solid. As he stumbled, he tried to jump, hurdling the object in his path, but he didn't make it. His trailing leg also caught on the blockage and sent him tumbling to the floor. He landed hard, tucked his head and tried to roll, his helmet flying free as he somersaulted through the air.

Pain shot through his head as he struck it on the ground, rolling twice as another pain flared in his arm. It started in his shoulder, then shot through his arm and out his fingers, as if he were the Emperor and the power of the dark side was ready to burst from his fingertips.

Justin laid there, his heart hammering in his chest, pain spotting his vision, ready for the end to come. That was when he saw the eyes staring at him, glistening with tears.

Zeke's large form, which had been the insurmountable obstacle in Justin's path, lay between him and death. The old man's face, under-lit by the light of the helmet which lay on the floor between them, reflected his own acceptance of death.

Justin hated himself for it, but he knew that it gave him a chance. He snatched at the helmet, and hauled himself to his feet as the first wave of baby cave spiders reached the man.

Justin replaced the helmet on his head and watched in horror as the spiders flooded over Zeke's massive frame. They obscured him from view with their numbers, tearing at his flesh until the man's blood seeped through their ranks.

An arm shot out of the pile, a hand largely stripped of flesh, and what remained hung loosely from the appendage like melted cheese hanging from a slice of pizza. The fingers stretched, reaching for the brothers in a silent cry for help.

"We can't help him." Declan was there once more, his hand on his brother's shoulders. "We need to move. The big ones are still here."

The words went some way toward shocking Justin back into life, and he allowed Declan to pull him along. They hurried into the darkness, unaware of what lay in wait for them, but certain that what they were leaving behind was a certain death.

"This way." Declan pulled his brother on one arm, and Justin altered his course. They moved as fast as they could, knowing that running was not a genuine option.

They could hear creatures continue to scurry behind them, but neither wanted to look for confirmation.

Justin felt something to his right, a rush of air, followed by a strange clicking sound. He dropped without thinking, grabbing at Declan in the process, both men hitting the ground hard. Before Declan could voice his surprise, they head the heavy thud of a third body landing close by.

A glance to their left, both helmet lights picked up on the thrashing form of a large cave spider. The creature was on its back, its legs wiggling frantically, as it tried to right itself. The stinger that had been so lethal when skewering the millipede flapped loose with each thrashing movement, while the creature's large, serrated front pincers slashed at the air, ready to fight off anything that came close to it while vulnerable.

"There, look," Declan said, as the light of the torch picked up on another large fissure in the rock.

"How do you know …?" Justin started, but stopped, interrupting his own question. "Never mind, I get it."

They charged towards the gap, scrambling over the uneven ground, plunging themselves into the tight crevice in the cave wall. A few seconds after they made it, the heavy impact of the cave spiders charging against the rock made them both yell.

"Keep going," Declan called, as he felt the serrated teeth rip a jagged tear through the shoulder of his jacket.

They were just out of reach, but the clacking sound of the excited bugs told him that they were not going to go away anytime soon. They needed to push on.

"It's too tight, there's no way we can make it," Justin growled as he twisted his head to the side and kept inching his way deeper.

"We don't have a choice," Declan answered, relieved to feel nothing but the gentle push of air as he moved beyond the range of the swiping, serrated mandibles.

"I can't breathe, it's too tight," Justin groaned, using the tips of his toes to drive himself deeper. The rock was dripping into his flesh and could feel the warm trickle of blood from the multiple lacerations the rough surface had carved into his back.

Justin stopped and closed his eyes. His chest was growing tight, not just from the pressure of the wall, but on the inside. He couldn't breathe and his skin itched. The multiple trickles of blood felt like the scurrying feet of bugs, crawling over his flesh. He began to feel light-headed, the power leaving his legs. Had it not been for the wall holding him snug, he would have fallen.

"Justin, you need to move," Declan whispered, keeping his voice low to not draw more attention from creatures, which appeared to have lost some interest in their hidden prey.

"I … I can't," Justin stammered. "They're all over me, Dec, I can feel them. Get them off me, Dec. Get them off."

"There's nothing, Justin, you need to move," Declan snapped back, as Justin began to panic.

His body thrashed against the rocks. He began to shriek, his screams triggering memories in Declan that he had long since learned to keep buried. Memories of his brother being locked away in the shed, his mother standing guard until his cries gave way to the faint that would always claim him.

"There's nothing. Just breathe, Justin, breathe," Declan said, trying to calm his brother whose breaths were coming faster and faster.

Declan knew what would come next. He couldn't let his brother pass out. He could barely breathe with the pressure of the rocks against his muscular chest. If they got trapped there, they would die.

"Justin, listen to me. Listen." Declan didn't want to raise his voice, but knew he needed to take a stern approach. "Listen, goddammit. We're trapped, and you need to move. You have to keep going, Justin."

Justin's body fell still, while a gargled breath escaped his lungs. His body slumped, falling into the clinging embrace of the cave.

"Justin," Declan called, raising his voice after receiving no response. "Justin, wake up."

The echo of his voice drew the attention of the cave spiders, who returned to the crevice, probing the gap with long-reaching, inquisitive pincers.

"Justin, come on, wake up." Declan's own mind was racing, trying to battle back against the encroaching waves of panic that were lapping at the shores of his mind.

Declan inched his way through the gap, and grabbed his brother and shook him as best he could given his limited room to work. He seized Justin's arm, and shook until he sprang back into consciousness with a jolt.

"Declan!" Justin's cry was laced with hysteria. He felt Declan's hand on his arm and freaked, thrashing and lashing out.

"Hey, hey, it's me, it's me." Declan brought his voice back down, and he was once again comforting his baby brother.

"Declan?" Justin spoke, his voice confused.

"It's me, brother. You need to get it under control. We can't stay here." Declan knew they couldn't waste time.

"I can't. It's too tight. I can't move," Justin cried.

"You have to try. Can't you feel that, the air? It's moving towards us, so there has to be a way out. You need to try, Justin."

"Okay, okay," Justin said, sounding less than confident, but it was a start, and Declan took it.

Slowly, inch by suffocating inch, the brothers moved deeper through the cave, their bodies crushed by the rocks, to the point where their breaths were little more than feeble gasps, taken so frequently to combat their shallow nature that they sweated from the exertion.

The sweat that streamed from them worked to their advantage, slicking the rocks and acting as a lubricant, offering them a modicum of assistance, until finally, like children being born into a new world, they were spat from the wall and fell to the floor, exhausted and unable to support themselves any longer.

On the floor, their overheated bodies spread flat, absorbing as much of the coolness from the ground as possible. They lay still, hyperventilating, hovering between consciousness and the soothing embrace of black nothing.

Declan still clutched his helmet in one hand, but he lacked the energy to turn it over and shed some light on their situation. His body ached and all he wanted was to lie still and let it be over. The trip through the cave had been downhill, taking them even deeper, and by that measure, even further away from escape.

"Justin, are you alive?" Declan asked, his voice weak and scratchy.

"I have no idea, man," Justin answered, pushing himself up to his knees.

He remained there for a few moments, teetering on the edge, trying to decide if he was going to vomit, collapse, or just stand up. After giving it considerable thought, Justin pushed himself to his feet, shaking his arms to try and dilute the lactic acid build up that was making them feel as if they were on fire.

Behind him, he heard Declan do the same. A few moments later, the glow of the helmet torch lit up the darkness, although the glass was cracked, and the light it gave seemed to be weaker than it had been earlier.

"We need to find a new light source," Declan said, holding the dying helmet in his hands.

"Maybe we will find a secret cache of torches," Justin said, trying to sound funny, but only succeeding to sound sarcastic and flippant. "Sorry."

"We need to keep moving," Declan said, ignoring both the comment and the apology.

The cavern was smaller than the previous ones, but the ground was wet. Dripping stalactites descended like fangs. Twisted rock formations dribbled water as if salivating at the prospect of the flesh that was trapped within its deep-buried borders.

The damp smell was heavy in the air, the taste of mildew coated the tongue with each deep breath. The ground was slippery in places, especially in the areas around the descending stalactite monstrosities, where the water pooled and eventually ran away, following the natural slope of the cave.

As they moved into the center of the chamber, they were able to look around and see the far side wall. Three tunnels sprang from the walls, each one large enough for a man to stand. None of them looked like a natural formation, their shape too uniform, and their spacing too even.

"Are you thinking what I'm thinking?" Declan asked as they moved closer.

"They look man-made," Justin said, staring at them with a sort of fascination.

"Yep."

"That means there has to be a way out," Justin said. Neither brother looked at one another; their words were spoken with a casual air, their overloaded minds not registering the full scope of what such a discovery could mean.

They moved across all three tunnels, trying to decide which one to take. As they stood, Justin spun around, looking back into the darkness. He felt as though he was being watched. He couldn't see a thing, the darkness of the cave was absolute, but the feeling made his skin crawl. They had to get out soon; otherwise, he was going to go crazy.

"Do you see that?" Declan took hold of his brother's arm, turning him back toward the caves.

"See what?"

"That. Look above the tunnels." Declan pointed, and Justin followed the beam of light from the helmet.

Across the top of each tunnel entrance, carved into the rock wall was some form of script. While they resembled English in some way, there were illegible and formed no recognizable words. Yet, there could be no mistake what they were.

"Labels," Justin said. "They are labels, probably giving the tunnels a name or a purpose." A shiver ran through his body, shrinking his flesh until it felt as if it would tear open at the seams. The hairs all over his body stood erect as the shudder passed, leaving him feeling violated and balanced even more precariously on the knife edge of sanity.

"That's what I'm thinking," Declan said, thinking back to the campfire story they had been told.

"You don't think this has anything to do with that town legend, do you?" Justin asked as if reading his brother's mind.

"I have no fucking idea, but this is some weird shit. We need to get out of here." For the first time since they fell, Justin heard the depth of fear in Declan's voice.

"I'm with you, but which tunnel do we take?" Justin stared at the black hole before them, the light of the helmet torch somehow failing to penetrate the thickness of the void.

"Well, put your hand up." Declan did the same and waited for Justin to follow. "You feel that?"

"Wind?" Justin said, confused.

"Two of them have a draught, and one, this one, seems to slope upwards, at the very start at least." Declan laid out all the things he had found and waited for Justin to catch up.

"Then let's take this one," Justin said as if the decision was a simple as which T-shirt to wear.

Declan nodded, the action indicated by the movement of the light beam.

Behind them, something moved in the darkness of the cavern. The clacking of feet and tumble of loose stone and rock got them moving down the tunnel double-time, their hearts thundering once again.

The tunnel was a close fit but seemed uniform in its size. They were able to walk upright, for the most part, only having to duck down at certain points where it looked as if the tunnel had partially collapsed. The longest they had to crawl was twenty meters or so. The ground beneath them was littered with debris, crushed rock, and smaller stones.

"What happened here?" Justin asked, his curiosity growing and providing a welcome distraction to the unyielding reality of their situation.

"I guess it was a collapse of some sort. Hey, check this out," Declan said.

They were on their feet again, and as Declan stretched his back, the torchlight picked up on something on the wall. It was a painting, much like the one he had seen before the bridge collapsed. It was clearly an image of three figures surrounding another. The fourth was on its knees, painted in red, unlike the others, whose fading outlines were black. They stood above a pit, or on a ledge. It was hard to tell. Beneath them were three large figures, which looked to be crude examples of women, with swollen bellies and breasts that overflowed their bodies. They were crowded together and looked to be staring up at the other men, as if in expectation, or want.

"What the heck?" Justin asked as he shuddered once again.

"This is some weird shit. You realize that we could be the very first people to see this. Outsiders, I mean." Declan spoke with a voice filled with wonder, intrigue winning out over fear.

"Wonderful," Justin replied, not even bothering to hide the barbed tone in his voice.

"Think about it. If that story was actually true, this could be the remains of the breakaway camp. We could be about to make the discovery of a lifetime." Declan clapped his younger brother on the shoulder. "It's amazing."

"Amazing?" Justin gasped in disbelief. "What the fuck is amazing about all of this?" He flung his arms out wide, both hands reaching opposite sides of the tunnel. "We're trapped, God knows how far underground, being chased by killer bugs that look like they belong in Chernobyl. What is amazing about this?'

Justin was panting by the time he finished his rant, and Declan waited a few moments before responding, giving his brother time to settle.

"Life's an adventure. One thing I learned I prison is that everything is an adventure if you approach it with the right mindset." Declan sounded like a preacher talking to his flock.

Justin gave a disbelieving grunt and turned away from his brother. "That's bullshit."

"You've never done time, so you wouldn't know," Declan snapped back.

"And what is that supposed to mean?" Justin felt his anger boiling over.

"Nothing, I just mean … well, look at you. You turned into a success story. You had it impossible when you were young, but after that, you had a good life. I guess you don't want for much, seeing how you live. That's great, and I'm happy for you, but you don't know what life is really like." Declan was calm, his words spoken with the passion of a speaker, up on stage, giving his message to the adoring crowd.

"So, you are blaming me for having a good life, is that what this is all about?" Justin snapped, his frustration boiling over with anger as old wounds split open once again, bubbling a black poison into his brain, convincing him that his brother held some deep-seated grudge against him.

Declan took a step back, shocked by the turn of the conversation.

"No, of course not. We've been through this. You need to let that go," Declan said.

"Let it go? I ruined your life, you spent your life in prison, branded as a murderer." Justin slapped his hand against the wet wall as he spoke, his rage building.

"I am a murderer. Whatever happened, whatever way you look at it, I am that. I killed Dad, and I would kill him again if it came to it, because it was what needed to be done. I made that choice, I knew what would happen. I don't blame you. I'm just trying to tell you that I learned a lot on the inside, and one is to take every day for what it is; a gift. I saw men die in prison. I saw people get people to the point where they spent the rest of their lives hooked up to machines. Life is fragile, and sure, we are trapped down here, but there is always going to be a way out. I choose to believe that." Justin shrank away from his brother as Declan built up a head of steam, his words not angry, but firm.

"So, what, you are happy you are trapped down here? Is that it?" Justin didn't know what to say. His head ached, his body felt alien to him, and he felt exhausted on levels he did not even know were possible.

"In a way, yes. I'm here, alive, and having an adventure with my baby brother. If you would have asked me a decade ago if you and I would ever be out on an adventure together, I would have laughed. We're in a tight spot, for sure, but this, these markings. They are a piece of history nobody knows about." Declan directed the light back towards the drawings, leaving Justin to ponder his words.

"I just want to get out of here. I've had enough adventure for one lifetime." Justin understood where Declan was coming from, but he could not bring himself to admit that they were anything other than fucked.

Just as the silence between them become comfortable, losing the awkward quality that Justin had planted and seen bloom, a shriek rang out from ahead of them, shattering everything.

The cry was long and punctuated by short periods of quiet and a dull hammering. It continued for a short while before the ensuing silence rolled over them like a mist out at sea. It enveloped them and only added to the mystery of what they had heard and the terror that they felt.

They moved forward, creeping slowly, not wanting to make a sound, they continued through the tunnel, eventually coming to the decimated corpse of what looked to be a large spider. The creature was easily the size of a Labrador, its legs broken and hanging disjointedly from its body. The large abdomen was split open, spilling pus-colored organs on a sea of black mulch, which leaked from the body with a consistency of cottage cheese.

The creature's legs were curled inwards, but occasionally one would straighten as if lashing out in the final throes of death.

"What the ...?" Justin began, when suddenly the light from Declan's helmet shifted away from the body, to the blood pool that was slowly spreading over the surrounding rock.

Justin watched and his heart froze in his chest as he saw what lead away from the creature's body.

"Declan," Justin began his words nothing but icy lumps in his mouth.

He didn't need to say anything further, because he saw the tremor in the beam of light, and heard Declan's fear-laden exhalations, shuddering releases of breaths held for too long.

Leading away from the body, tracking through the blood were footprints, oddly misshapen but clearly human in origin.

The heel print, the ball of the foot, and then the imprint of toes clearly marked in blood, hurried deeper into the darkness.

"Declan," Justin repeated, his mind unable to conjure any other word. His heart still felt as if it refused to beat, and the sweat that had covered his body had now frozen, leading him to shudder.

"Maybe … maybe it's not what it looks like," Declan said, his words about as convincing as a used car salesman during a late-night advert break.

"Yeah, maybe," Justin said, his eyes locked on the prints. "We're hurt, exhausted, we are seeing things."

"Exactly." Neither brother truly believed what they were saying, but there was a comfort to be found in the shared lie, a twisted understanding that if others bought into it, then surely there was a chance that it was true.

They stared at the footprints until the trail became dry, the creature behind them dead, and starting to stink, the odor rising from its stinking carcass already attracting the first round of bugs to the feast. With little option but to keep moving, they set off, making their way through the dark, the light firmly focused on the floor now, as if they were tracking the fleeing figure, rather than praying they could avoid making contact with it.

The tunnel continued on in an upward gradient, hitting moments of a steep incline that made it hard for walking. Once again, the walls began to expand around them and feed them into another large chamber, only this one was far from empty.

The ground was littered with bones, both in the form of fully complete skeletons as well as individual bones ripped from bodies and casually discarded. The stench of death was heavy in the air, and as they stood in horror, their backs pressed hard against the walls of the cave, both Declan and Justin saw fresher kills, with rotting meat still sitting on the festering corpses.

There were spiders and bugs, and four-legged creatures of a range of shapes and sizes. Clothing lay strewn about the carnage as if ripped from struggling bodies in the eager quest for meat.

There was a savagery that hung in the room, and the screams of those long since dead still seemed to echo around. It was a chamber of horrors, hidden beneath the surface of the world, a place where cruelty reigned supreme and compassion was a concept never heard before.

"What the hell is this place?" Justin asked.

"It's their meat locker," Declan replied.

Justin snapped his head up to look at his brother, ready to admonish him for a poor taste and timing in using humor, only he saw from Declan's face that he was not joking. They were inside the meat locker of whatever lived in the caves. They were trapped inside a hellish reality; the stuff late-night movies were made of. Only their blood would not be corn syrup, it would be real, and if they were not careful, it would be spilled by the bucket load.

They carefully picked their way around the edge of the cave, pausing as they stepped over the remains of a young girl, her body a heap, the legs stripped of flesh and meat, the bones beneath scratched and scarred with deep gouges. A crack ran along the length of her left femur, and black marrow had bubbled up through the fault, spilling over the bone, staining it like rot.

"Look," Declan said, staring at the body, the remaining flesh of her torso shining blue under the light of the torch.

"I'd rather not," Justin said, feeling his stomach churn, the acidic taste of vomit rising in his mouth while saliva flooded his mouth in an effort to help wash away the looming pre-taste of what was to come.

"No, look. She's fresh, but look at her chest." Declan held the light on the girl, who could not have been more than late teens if she was a day.

There could be no mistaking the crudely stitched up lines of the Y-incision that had sliced across the top of her breasts and down towards her pelvis. The stitching was cheap, the job rushed, with no care or attention given to the girl.

"That's from an autopsy," Justin said, finally realizing what his brother had been trying to tell him.

"Exactly, so that means somebody is actually dumping bodies down here." Declan looked at his brother, blinding him with the light from the helmet.

"To hide them?" Justin asked.

"To feed them," Declan added, his words inducing another shiver that thickened Justin's blood to the point of freezing. His entire body ached from the pain of pushing semi-solidified blood through his veins. He felt as if he might split open, a fitting end to join the pile of the dead they had just discovered.

"Who are they?" Justin found strength in his words, realizing that if he kept his mind busy, he gave himself less chance to focus on the horror of their situation.

Declan turned around, leaving Justin in near darkness, giving him a moment to realize that the sea of bones was reflecting the light and actually helping him see more of the cavern. He shuddered and moved closer to Declan.

Declan took a sharp breath, a painful sound that brought Justin's heart to a stop. "Holy shit, would you look at that,"

"What?" Justin asked, his eyes seeing the etchings just as he spoke.

The walls around them were covered in paintings and symbols. Most looked more like hieroglyphics than anything else, but there was something about their structure that made Justin feel as though he could somehow read them, or at least glean a modicum of understanding from them.

His eyes moved over the figures. The stick images were crude, yet when viewed as a whole they created scenes. Each scene appeared to correspond to the image closest to them.

"It's a story," Justin said, as he felt his mind getting drawn deeper into the imagery.

"You can read this?" Declan asked, surprised.

"No, but ... well, it kind of reminds me of my first job in tech. I was coding for some shitty piece of software, and none of it made sense. Not just because I was new, but because the code was a mess. But you had the code in the back end, and the screens the users see. If you look at it from both sides, then things started to make a little more sense. This is kind of like that. Here, take a look at these." Justin pointed up to the closest group of pictures that showed a circle of stick figures surrounding a central figure that seemed to be lying prone on the ground before them. "That text there goes with this image, and it moves into this one here."

The next image showed the prone figure in pieces, the head, legs, and arms pulled apart, while the heads of those surrounding it were painted a rust-tinted red.

"They cut up and ate that man. Sacrificed him, maybe. The symbols would tell us if only we could actually read them." Justin's eyes moved slowly over the walls, the intrigue into the macabre story they told distracting his mind from the horrors that surrounded them, as if reading about the hall somehow made it a work of fiction and thus removed the truth from the floor around them.

"You don't think that this is them, do you?" Declan asked, once again turning to look at his brother.

"Who?" Justin looked at Declan confused.

"Them, that camp of people that got chased away back when people were first settling here," Declan said. "The ones Ben and Trevor told us about?"

Justin gave a laugh. It was a sudden and unexpected reaction, and it felt extremely alien to him. "That was just a campfire ghost story."

"Really, then how do you explain a cave full of bones, a mother-fucking corpse that's had a full autopsy done on it, and all of these drawings." Declan spoke faster and faster, his voice rising in pitch as his nerves finally started to break through the thick wall he held them all behind.

Justin paused, unsure how to answer it. Declan had pulled him out of the theory that it was all just in his head and rooted him back into the sobering present.

"Well ... that was hundreds of years ago," Justin started, but stopped as the light of the helmet began to flicker.

Declan shook the helmet and the light came back on. He held it in his hands at an angle that highlighted the wall higher up than they had been looking. What the beam highlighted left no doubt in their minds, for there could be no confusing the lettering there. Crawleigh was spelled in large block capitals, the dye used long since faded, but what remained was as clear to the brothers as a lighthouse beacon on a misty night.

Justin opened his mouth and swallowed, his throat suddenly as dry as the morning after a heavy drinking session.

He spun around as something caused the bones behind them to clatter. They head the pattering of footsteps, but the darkness offered them nothing. By the time Declan had the helmet spun around, there was nothing.

"It's nothing. Just our imaginations running wild," Declan told his brother, but it was clear from his tone that he didn't believe himself either.

That's when the darkness laughed at them, a high-pitched, child-like laugh; dainty and carefree. Both looked up and saw the figure standing at the entrance to the central tunnel. It looked like a little girl, but the instant the light pick up on her form, she turned and ran. Her movements were skittish and somewhat disjointed, but there could be no denying that she was not a bug.

"Hey," Declan called out.

"What the hell are you doing?" Justin gasped, lashing out with a backhand across Declan's arm.

"She could help us find a way out," Declan said.

Justin gave an irritated snort before answering, "If they knew a way out, do you really think they would still be living underground?"

Declan ignored his brother's snide remarks and kept his voice as level as possible. "Those bodies got down here somehow. Either they went up and got them, or someone delivered them here. Either way, they know how to get out."

Justin didn't realize it, but they were walking after the girl whether he liked it or not. It was only when they entered the tunnel and the walls closed in around him again that he realized what was going on.

The tunnel was tight, and he needed to stoop down in order to walk through. Etchings and images covered the walls, like modern-day graffiti; images and characters, words and lines of text. They covered the rock, overlapping each other with no real sense of continuity. Unlike the story being told in the bone chamber, this was a jumble built up over the years and the centuries.

"Wait for a second," Justin said before they had moved too far away from the chamber.

"What?" Declan asked.

"We should arm ourselves … just in case." Justin looked back toward the chamber.

"That might not be a bad idea," Declan said, giving the first indication of the fear he felt coursing through his veins.

Returning to the chamber, they each grabbed a femur, and after testing them for signs of a break or decomposition, or anything else that may impact the integrity of their weapons, they returned to the pursuit.

They could not hear the girl, the echo of her laugh long since extinguished, but they would follow the tunnel in whatever direction it took them. They had no plan but knew they were running out of options. The trail of dead behind them was motivation enough to keep moving forward.

The tunnel moved at a steady incline, which had their muscles burning with the buildup of lactic acid, their tired bodies struggling under the new demand.

Justin carried his bone weapon in two hands and strongly considered letting it fall completely, his body ready to stop.

Then each time, he thought of his kids. Their faces popped into his head, and they gave him the motivation to continue. He thought of his wife and how she had rescued him. But then the dark thoughts came, riding on the coattails. Her drinking problem, the way it had become just a normal part of their lives. It hung over Justin like a black cloud, knowing he had facilitated it for so long. Sure they had argued about it, and she had tried rehab and meetings a couple of times, but each time she would break again, blaming the past, and he would let her get away with it.

Both light and dark thoughts bolstered him. He was determined to see his family again and determined to do things right. He would fix the problems, fix the real issues, the ones that money could not solve or bury.

Then, as his will to survive rose up, his determination pushing the last ounces of adrenaline through his body, he looked over and saw Declan.

He saw his brother, who was alone in the world, who had sacrificed so much, and continued to push on, to strive towards a new tomorrow.

The emotions were strong and confusing. They swirled around inside his brain and left his head aching even more, the steady beat inside his skull strong enough to tear through the blood-soaked wrapping, or so it felt.

"Do you smell that?" Declan spoke first, ending the silence of the tunnel and silencing the voices in Justin's head.

"I smell something, and I don't like it," Justin said, the odor filtering through to his brain.

The stench of wet rot and sewage was heavy on the air, thick as if it was a physical presence that was attacking them. It coated every breath, tainting them with its overpowering aroma. They could taste it every time they swallowed and could feel it settling on their skin like a fine rain, seeping into their bodies like a toxin.

"We must be getting close to something," Declan mused.

They carried on down the tunnel, ignoring the stench of rot that surrounded them until they reached a fork in the road.

"Maybe –"

"Don't even fucking suggest it," Justin interrupted Declan before he could even finish starting to speak. "We are not splitting up."

Declan was quiet for a moment before nodding. "True, we've only got one light."

After choosing the right-hand fork, they moved on, and when the tunnels split again, they went to the right once more. They had no basis for their decision, but both moved without hesitation down the same fork, and so they rolled with it.

They had seen no sign of the girl, but it was clear they were still in the warren constructed by the original Crawleigh family because the walls were still covered in markings.

"There has to be something," Justin said, frustration beginning to conquer the fear. He was tired, and his body longed to rest, his spirit begging him to sit and let his wounds heal up some. All he wanted to do was sleep.

"Let's just keep going," Declan said, exhaustion clear in his voice also.

When the light went out for the third time in as many minutes, it took several attempts to get it to work again. Justin, who had taken control as he was the one walking at the head of their small procession, slammed it against his hand, cursing under his breath, when suddenly a fading yellow beam appeared, the color a dull and dirty shade, indicative of how tired they were.

Justin squinted and turned the light away from him, highlighting the features that were standing inches from his face.

Milk-colored blind eyes faced his direction, set in the center of a pasty, hairless face. The skin was a wet grey coloration, with open sores and weeping lesions covering it, dripping on opaque liquid, which glinted on the skin, leaving a snail-like trail of putrescence behind. The head was unusually long, with one ear torn vertically through the middle, flapping uselessly to one side, while the other was missing completely, a rotting hole, a bubbling black mass of weeping tissue all that remained.

Justin gasped, but Declan's hand appeared and covered his mouth. The creature was inches from them, yet did not seem to realize they were there.

Its body shook as it took wet, rasping breaths, shallow and quick, like a dog in the sun. Its body was lacking any real signs of muscle or power. It looked soft and dough-like. Yet it dragged a bone club behind it, the ball joint on the killing end stained brown with blood.

The creature sniffed the air and opened its mouth wide, revealing black, near-toothless gums with wriggling maggots filling the crevices where teeth should have been. Its breath was foul and made Justin gag, and as terror overwhelmed him, he lost all control. He felt the warm stream of piss travel down his leg, and as soon as the aroma hit the air, the creature changed.

Its eyes narrowed and its nose twitched. Snarling, it lunged forward. Reacting fast, Declan hauled Justin backward.

The creature fell to the floor, dropping down onto its hands and feet. Its body cracked as its joints moved in ways that seemed wholly unnatural as it lowered itself to the floor.

It sniffed the puddle of urine before a long black tongue descended and began lapping at the pungent, yellow liquid.

Seeing the creature, knowing that they were more of them, Justin felt something rise up inside him, disgust and anger that he had not felt in many years. It was resentment at the way his life had gone. It was everything that had happened to him and been stored away; the sessions and the counseling. Sure, he had talked about the abuse, he had confessed, but it had done nothing to extinguish the fire, the burning hatred that had been etched into him. Flaring now, the fires consumed him as he watched some abomination drinking his piss from the floor. It was the final straw, the final thing anybody would take from him.

With a battle cry that startled the human-like creature, Justin brought his femur weapon down onto the things head. The wet thud, like a rotten twig snapping in half, was not as satisfying as he had hoped. The blow stunned the creature, opening up a long wound on the back of its head, thick blood bubbling to the surface.

Justin raised the club again and brought it down, driving it into the squirming creature's skull. It gave a shrill, squawked cry as its head burst from the force of the impact. Globs of grey brain matter oozed through the gaping wound, but it was not enough to satisfy Justin's sudden blood lust. Striking again and again, Justin growled, the blood splashing up to cover his face with a black mask of gore.

"Hey, hey, that's enough," Declan said, wrapping his arms around his brother, stopping him from striking out again.

The creature's head was gone, reduced to nothing more than a messy pulp on the floor, as if someone had dropped an overripe melon and then kicked it for good measure.

The body still twitched, somehow, but there would be no coming back, that was for sure.

Justin stood, panting, his lungs and arms burning from the exertion, but he would not stop. The anger had taken control and would drive him further for as long as he could control it.

Stepping over the creature, Justin strode forward, the gore-dripping bone held in his hands like a shotgun.

"I get it now," Justin said as they walked.

"Get what?" Declan asked, still trying to get over the shock of what he had seen.

"Why you killed Dad. I get it." Justin's words were emotionless, and that sent a chill up Declan's spine that felt worse than anything else he had experienced until that moment.

"I didn't feel good for killing him," Declan said, speaking directly about the act that changed their lives, for the first time.

"You didn't?" Justin asked, disbelieving.

"No, I live with that decision every day," Declan answered, his jaw clenched as he spoke.

"He got what he deserved. You did the right thing, you said it yourself," Justin answered, nonchalantly.

"I said I would do the same thing again, and I would. It doesn't make it the right choice though. That's one thing I know for sure. I didn't get a fancy education, but I know that people don't deserve to say when another man's time is up." Declan didn't want to get into that discussion, and so he held his tongue on the rest.

"Nonsense. He was a bully and an abuser. He deserved to die, and he deserved to feel pain," Justin growled.

Declan ignored the words, knowing it was the stress that was talking, not his baby brother. Yet, there was a deep-seated anger that he recognized.

Before he had a chance to bring it up again, there were a series of shrieks in the tunnel behind them, too close for comfort.

"I think they found your handiwork," Declan said as he pushed Justin into a run.

The shrieks and cries echoed through the tunnel were accompanied by the sound of running feet, which rose like thunder around them.

"Move, quick, quick," Declan yelled as the chasing group drew closer to them. The sound of grunts and feet slapping the wet ground seemed to rumble, the echo of the cavern and the tunnels made it sound as if they were surrounded and being closed in on rather than chased down.

"Run," Declan yelled, the time to quiet was long since over. Declan could hear the pack getting closer, and he refused to end up another pile of bones in their meat locker.

Ahead of them, the tunnel forked.

"Left," Justin called back to his brother as his feet stumbled on the floor. He pinwheeled with his arms to keep both his balance and speed, careening into the tunnel absorbed by the darkness.

Tripping, his balance refusing to hold for him, Justin fell towards the wall. He tried to bring his hands up to protect himself, only there was no wall. He was falling through empty space, the ground disappearing beneath his feet.

With no idea of how far he had to fall, Justin's head conjured up the worst image it could think of. Justin saw himself falling only to land only a group of rising skewers of rock. He saw his body pierced and impaled, his guts caught on the tip, yanked from his body like wool on a spindle.

He opened his mouth to scream, but the floor was there. Hitting face first and unable to brace for the impact, his body was not prepared for the sudden stop. The pain registered as he landed, his nose splattering like a squeezed grape. It saw his world light up with pain before the darkness swam back in to claim him.

Declan saw his brother stumble and disappear into the darkness. "Justin," he called out but got no response.

The light of the helmet bounced around furiously as Declan ran, giving him little or no vision of what lay ahead. He was simply running. The pack was still getting closer to him, but he didn't want to chance a glance over his shoulder.

Hoping he would run into his brother, Declan continued, when suddenly something hit him in the stomach. The blow came from nowhere, originating from the right-hand side. At first, he thought he had been stabbed, as the pain flared up like fire, consuming his gut and sweeping through his body. Lurching forward, his body useless, Declan felt hands grab him, tearing at what remained of his clothes. He was shoved to his right, hitting the wall hard, his head whipping to the side, catching the rocks. Stars exploded before his eyes, and he felt blood start to flow from the wound that had opened above his ear.

They surrounded him, their grunts and chats bearing no resemblance to English. Declan tried to look up, but couldn't. Crawling on the floor, he hid the light beneath him, hoping the darkness would buy him some cover. Crawling, he felt the ground give way beneath him, and he gave himself to the fall, welcoming the descent and whatever impact laid waiting for him.

The shouts and grunts came again, and Declan heard something behind him. He hit the floor too soon after leaving it, the drop was not more than a few meters. Rolling as best he could, reacting after the initial impact had occurred, he felt his shoulder burn and head the pop as it dislocated.

Declan gritted his teeth against the pain, and tried to find his bearings. His stomach still burned from whatever had struck him, but he felt no blood as he ran his hands over his shirt. Still holding his bone club in one hand, he hauled himself to his feet, using it like a cane.

It didn't take long for Declan to realize he wasn't alone. Even in the dim light offered by the helmet, which lay on the ground behind him, Declan could tell.

He felt something moving through the air. Not wanting to put it down to his imagination, he grabbed the bone like a bat and swung it as hard as he could. He would not go down without a fight.

CHAPTER THIRTEEN

The club connected with something solid, forcing a rush exhalation from the creature's lungs. The rotten breath expelled hit Declan in the face, and like the musk of a skunk, it was strong enough to drive him backward.

Stumbling a step, he listened, but couldn't react in time to stave off the second figure that attacked him.

Hands wrapped around his face, long nails digging into his flesh. The stench of rot filled every breath as slimy skin slipped over his face, smothering him. An exploratory finger found his mouth and slid inside. Declan gagged, the taste and smell of the greasy digit too much for him. A sharp nail gouged a strip of flesh from his tongue, and Declan bit down, instinctively. His teeth severed the flesh and bone of the finger, which was far too soft.

A thick, sour-tasting liquid filled his mouth, causing vomit to rise from his gut. It exploded from his mouth like when a Mentos gets thrown into a coke bottle. The foaming liquid that his body created was unlike any vomit Declan had produced before.

Behind them, the first creature had gotten from the floor and was upon him within seconds. Arms wrapped around him, but Declan was ready. He would not go down without a fight, and so he threw himself forward, bending at the waist, sending the creature hurtling over his back and onto the floor. Grabbing the bone, Declan held the club end and stabbed forward, impaling the thing through the shoulder.

The creature wailed and thrashed about, its screams increasing before suddenly, they became a laugh; a high-pitched, maniacal laugh. The creature snatched the bone out of Declan's hands and yanked it free with a wet, smacking sound.

It inspected the blood-covered bone, and smiled before it proceeded to lick the bone clean, chewing the thicker lumps of gore as it reached them.

Declan gagged as the long black tongue picked the lumps of flesh and blood from the bone, Declan turned to run, but the second creature was on him again, it's teeth sinking deep into his shoulder, tearing loose a large lump of fresh meat. It was Declan's turn to howl with pain, and he did so gladly, dropping to his knees as the pain surged through him. He could hear the thing chewing on the bite he had taken. He could hear the crunch of his raw flesh as it was hungrily wolfed down.

"Please," Declan begged on his knees, nowhere else left to turn. "Let my brother go." The two creatures looked at each other as if they could understand what was being asked of them.

One stood, his face caked in fresh blood and a goofy smile on his face; the other stood with the bone club in its hands, a look of cold calculation in its eyes. The blood-smeared creature crouched down onto its haunches and pushed its face to within a few inches of Declan's. Its eyes stared into his, and the goofy smiled disappeared as it opened its mouth, as if making to speak.

"No." It managed to force the word from its lips before standing back up as both broke down into a fit of hysterical laughter.

"No, no, no, no," the bloody beast repeated over and over, its voice hoarse but clear. It started to bounce around, its excitement building, while its companion stood, staring at Declan with cold eyes. The time for laughter was done.

The thing raised the club above its head, and swung in a strike not dissimilar to Declan's own. The strike was fast, and Declan didn't even have the time to raise his hand to protect himself. The bone hit hard, his head exploding from the force of the blow, sending him to the ground.

Declan was unconscious before he finished his fall.

***

Justin came to and all he knew was pain. His world exploded anew with each breath he took. Trying to move only increased his agony to a new level he did not previously know existed. Yet above the pain, he heard something ... several somethings.

He heard his brother scream. He knew it was Declan. He could recognize the sound of his brother's agony anywhere. It sounded exactly as it had in every nightmare he had had since the day Declan was arrested.

"No," he mumbled, his broken lips blurring the words into an indistinguishable sound.

Justin didn't know if it was adrenaline or something else, some power from a higher authority, but a surge of energy kicked in, shutting down his pain, bringing him to his feet. His head throbbed, and all he could taste was blood, as it poured from his shattered nose and mangled mouth. He turned around, trying to find his bearings, but it was dark. Holding his arms out, he felt the wall. Moving against it, flinching at each bump and crack, with visions of bugs and beasts dancing in his head, Justin felt upwards, searching for the entrance he had fallen through. There was nothing and no clear way to reach up any higher.

He was trapped. His first thought turned to a holding cell, where they would keep their food. He stopped to rest for a moment, closing his eyes while he waited for a moment of light-headedness to pass.

He turned around, looking to the cave wall for support. He fought back tears as the bitter fingers of desperation grabbed at the edges of his sanity, trying to wrench it away, removing his comforter before exposing him to the true depths of the hell he had stumbled into.

At first, he thought the light was a spot on his vision. A sign of the obvious concussion he had picked up since the day began, if it was even still the same day. He had lost all concept of time since falling from the bridge.

He blinked several times, first fast, and then slower, but the light remained, a hazy orange glow, originating not from within whatever chamber or cavern he had landed in, but from somewhere else. Justin refused to let his hopes get ahead of him. Lights meant people. People meant a lost colony of presumed cannibals that were hunting him down, but he also knew that it meant visibility and the possibility of a way out.

Justin's legs trembled as he walked, as if still in deliberation as to whether they were going to hold him upright, Justin moved towards the glow.

He stood on something, and head it crack underfoot. It was the sound of eggshells. Without a light to see by, he could not check to see what else was in the chamber, and so he refused to let his racing mind ponder the thought for too long.

With his eyes focused on the orange glow, Justin made it across to chamber, which could not have been more than twenty feet wide. He found himself at the entrance to a tunnel. A small tight space dug into the wall. Blindly, he felt is way around the entrance and reasoned he should be able to crawl through it, because standing was not an option.

Ignoring the screaming inside his head, Justin forced his body onward. He moved on hands and knees, dropping down to his belly in a slow commando crawl not long after.

A strange stench wafted towards him, coming down the tunnel from whatever lay at the other end. It was a heady concoction that made Justin think of an old gym bag and compost. It had a strange, peaty, earth-like smell, rotting leaves, and body odor. It was slick yet lingered like old sweat, a constant stench rather than something passing on the breeze.

It increased as he inched his way closer to the end, and with it came a sound too; a wet, crawling sound. Justin couldn't place it anywhere, but knew it was the sound of multiple things, be it bugs or the original residents of Crawleigh.

Shadows began to dance on the tunnel wall as the eerie orange glow began to envelop him, the stench an unforgiving entity, as if he had crawled into the bowels of a fresh cadaver, just as the gasses were starting to build.

Justin wanted to turn back, but the tight confines made it impossible. His body was tired, and he hurt all over. Blood still dripped from the facial wounds, although the heaviest flow seemed to have stopped. He breathed through his mouth, gulping down as much air as he could each time, Justin edged closer, peering as if somehow he could zoom his vision and take a look around before his body arrived.

He saw a flame, naked and dancing on the wall, enticing him to come further, its hypnotic flickering tempting him closer, where he knew there would be warmth, and warmth brought comfort.

Justin reached the end of the tunnel, and stared into the room. He could not stifle the gasp that escaped his lips as his eyes took in the monstrosities that sat before him. The room was filled with women. Only they were nothing like anything he had seen before. They say equally spaced around the room, their bodies chained to the wall and floor, via cuffs that clamped down hard on their wrists and ankles. Naked, their enormous bodies looked to be swollen to the point of bursting, their bellies distended, the skin stretched so thin Justin believed he could see through it if he stared long enough. Large boils and swollen pustules covered their flesh around the different cuffs holding them in place, while open sores dotted the body of two. They looked weak, their eyes closed and heads lolling to one side as if unconscious.

The floor was thick with piss and shit, both fresh and dried, from where the women would defecate where they sat. Their breasts hung from their bodies, sliding over their bellies, nothing more than shapeless sacks of flesh.

Children scurried around them, moving on all fours like animals, their bodies deformed, limbs that bent at unnatural angles, faces contorted by genetic mutation and abnormalities. Some had only one eye, others two but were sightless as a result. They played in the filth, rolling with one another like bear cubs on a nature documentary.

Several sucked from the hanging tits of their mothers, nipples hanging a few feet above the floor where children could stop off and drink at will without needing to leave the game for too long.

All around the chamber old-fashioned oil lamps were burning, including one to Justin's immediate right. A moment spent close to it confirmed to him that they were also a cause of the stench, so it did not lay fully on the poor hygiene of the breeders below him.

Justin knew what he was a looking at: a breeding room of some kind. It sickened him, and yet his eyes lingered with a strange and morbid fascination. He thought of his own kids and the life they had had; a life of privilege, compared to his own upbringing. He felt for the children here; the women too. There was no way any of them were part of the original family, for their history was hundreds of years ago. They were merely people, humans, caught in a life cycle started long before they were born, and destined to continue living until their bodies finally withered and died. They were no more capable of fighting back or breaking the cycle than he had been all those years ago. His abusers were his parents, haunted by whatever unspoken horrors had been inflicted upon them, while theirs was the cave and the ghosts of ancestors long since claimed by the past.

Justin thought of his brother, lost somewhere inside the cave. Once again, he had led his brother away from the chance of a good life to ease his own selfish regret. Lost in thought, Justin stumbled, his hand slipping on the edge of the tunnel. The crash of his body against the tunnel echoed through the breeding room and brought everything to a sudden halt.

Justin held his breath as he felt the weight of dozens of pairs of eyes turning towards him, finding him in the gloom with a laser focus.

The women began to scream, their throats producing a gargled cry that seemed to be an attempt at speech. The children turned towards him, their teeth bared like wild dogs ready to attack.

One leaped at the opening and Justin pulled himself out of the way just in time. Another tried, leaping up into the entrance of the tunnel. They were the perfect height to move through it, and Justin wondered if the chamber he had been in was some sort of dormitory for them.

The small creature, which he could not associate with a child, advanced on him. Justin lashed out, his survival instinct kicking in. The creature stumbled backward and fell to the floor, landing with a puppy-like yelp. It turned and looked over at Justin just as another jumped up, razor-like claws scratching at the air, ready to slice through his flesh.

Justin reacted on instinct, plucking the creature from the air, his fist locking around the thing's head, Justin growled as he pulled it towards him with such a force there was nothing the toddler-sized miscreation could do. It slammed face first into the lip of the tunnel, his head denting inwards, the skull caving in on itself, driving both the nose and the eyes deeper into the skull. The creature wailed and struggled, and as Justin let it drop to the floor, he watched in wonder as the others turned on it, eliminating the weakest of the pack to keep the rest of them strong.

It was the chance he needed. Justin tumbled to the floor, riding what he felt had to be the very last of his energy reserves, as he ran towards the women. He had seen a tunnel behind them, one large enough for him to move through at little more than a crouch.

Fat arms reached for him as their screams increased until it sounded as if a herd of pigs had been stuck in the gut and left to bleed to death.

He leaped over two, their bulbous frames preventing them from posting much of a threat, other than their incessant screaming.

The tunnel was close, but one female stood between him, her arms reaching for him, the look on her face not one of fear, but delight. The look in her eyes one of rabid hunger. Drool flowed from her mouth like a river as the mere thought of plunging her teeth into his juicy flesh set her senses on overload.

Justin moved fast, grabbing another one of their young by the leg, swinging him like a mace, its head impacting against the side of its mother's skull. The small creature fell still and limp, while the mother's face tore open like damp crepe paper. Her bulk toppled from the impact, and she tottered on one point for a few moments, her panic serving to produce the momentum needed for her to topple over.

Her bulk hit the floor and the cries began anew, louder now. The young had finished feasting on their injured brother and turned on him once more, ready to protect their mothers until the very end.

Cursing his luck, Justin realized the fallen woman was now an even bigger impediment that she had been when righted. Moving as fast as his broken body would allow, he reached her and kicked out, the toe of his shoe catching her in the face, splitting her lips and inflicting wounds that came close to mirroring those gouged into his own face. Using her head as a step, Justin boosted himself over her frame, ignoring the way her skull seemed to give way beneath his foot, the same way muddy ground would when trodden on.

Justin forced his way into the tunnel, pushing through the thick cobweb that hung just over the threshold, like a fine curtain. Disoriented, he flung his arms out, finding support from the wall on both sides, Justin paddled his hands, helping propel himself through the tunnel faster as the snarls of the chasing pack grew louder.

The lighting in the cave continued to increase, and as Justin spilled into the large cavern, he stopped, his breath taken from him by the grand scale of what he saw. He waited almost too long, reacting just at the last moment, diving behind a large boulder that sat to the left of his position.

He couldn't do anything else, for the cave was full of Crawleigh's finest residents. Sinking to the floor, pressing his back against the rock to the point of pain, Justin closed his eyes, hugged his knees to his chest and waited for the inevitable.

The creatures would surely see the young, hear of his bloody rampage, and they would come for him.

Justin shook while tears stung his eyes as he thought about his family; about never seeing them again, about what they would think of his not returning. Would his body ever be found, or would he simply rot in the meat locker, surrounded by the bones of those that had also lost the fight?

He heard a commotion and tensed. The young were spilling into the chamber, their squeals echoing around him. Only, they didn't come for him. They should have already tasted his flesh. He opened his eyes as a series of screams rang out. He flinched, but managed to hold in his own cry of alarm.

As he peered around the boulder, Justin watched as the adults hurried down from the walls, scurrying like ants to face off against their young. Many simply jumped from a savage height, their bodies absorbing the heavy impact, which would have shattered the knees of any normal human being.

One raised a crudely fashioned ax and with a cry brought the weapon down on the head of one of the youngsters, splitting it down to the neck. Pulling the blade free, it licked the brain matter off and appeared to take a moment to savor the taste.

Panic spread fast, and soon the young were hurrying back into the tunnel, speeding towards their mothers. Many made it, but several were not so lucky. Turned on by the adults in their community, they were butchered, torn apart and feasted upon, as if they were infidels caught behind enemy lines rather than the future generation of their society.

With the young driven back, chased away to the safety of their breeding room, Justin watched as the adults returned to the walls. They walked upright, or close to it, their spines seemed to all carry the same heavy curve, giving them almost a hunchback-like appearance. Justin stared as they ascended the walls, which he noticed were covered with ladder-like constructions.

Each rung was made of bone, tethered together against more bone, tied together by thick ropes of hair. From his position behind the boulder, Justin did not have an unobstructed view of the chamber, but he saw enough to know that the ladders stretched up to varying heights, each one rising to a tunnel entrance.

One by one, they all disappeared, scurrying into the tunnels, going about whatever business it was that they saw tended each day.

Once Justin was sure the coast was clear, he hobbled out from behind the boulder and stood looking up at the ladders. He knew that freedom was up there. If he could get up high enough, there would be tunnels leading him outside. Declan was right, they had to be interacting with somebody above ground, otherwise, there was no way they could have survived for so long.

He studied the ladders, aware that he was wasting time standing around and that he would be exposed for the entire time he was climbing, Justin made a decision and started to climb. The bone rungs made for a hard climb, and he almost fell when one step broke as he put his weight down. He bit down and swallowed the scream as he felt a splinter of bone pierce the broken sole of his shoe and the flesh of his foot just beyond.

Suspended in the air, hugging the ladder as if it would somehow offer him more protection, Justin froze. He was running away while his brother was still down there. He had no way of knowing Declan was gone, and he refused to abandon him again. He didn't say anything when they were kids, not when the cops came, not during the trial. That guilt had eaten away at him for years, and he would not make the same mistake now.

Justin took a second to steel himself before he climbed back down. He hit the floor and looked around. He could hear the grunts and calls of the Crawleigh natives echoing around him. He had to move fast.

He picked out the tunnel the young had emerged from. He did not want to go back down there. He also reasoned that Declan would most likely be in that direction because they had both been moving in the same direction.

He picked the tunnel to the left of him, grabbing a lantern from the wall as he limped on. Unarmed and terrified, he was ready to go down swinging.

The tunnel was empty and opened into another larger chamber with three sub-tunnels sprouting from it. The maze-like conditions were a testament to the people that lived there, for Justin had no idea where they were or from where they had come.

The first thing he noticed as he raised the lantern was that this chamber, and the entrance to the tunnels, was unlike the others they had been in. This was old, and it had been made for a purpose. Wooden jousts and supports had been set into and against the walls, and what looked like the tracks of a mining system could be made out on the floor also.

"Well, I'll be damned," Justin said under his breath as he looked up onto the wall behind him, completing his inspection of the room.

Three skeletons hung on the wall, their bones dull and yellowed by age. A few thin strips of fabric clung to their bones, while a pile of dust, leather belts lay on the ground beneath them.

That was when Justin saw it. Something caught his eye, on the ground beneath the leather. Justin bent down to take a closer look. He picked the object up and felt as if his odds at surviving had increased. A sword. Not as sharp as it once had been, and a little beaten by age, but it was still a sword. Gripping it, Justin felt a surge of confidence rise up inside him.

It disappeared when he heard his brother's scream.

CHAPTER FOURTEEN

Declan came to and immediately his mind alerted him to the danger. When his body tried to move in reaction, his mind alerted him to the agony that was his wrecked body.

He tried to remember what had happened.

He had been jumped. He remembered the clubbing blow to his stomach. Ice-like pain that had shot through him had now given way to a heavy ache.

He rolled onto his belly, before rising to his knees and eventually his feet, testing each body part as he transitioned from one position to another. The world swam around him, the same way it did after a couple of beers and a shot of something stronger, only Declan knew he had not been drinking. The insanity that had become his life was as real as the burden he carried around on his soul.

This was his just desserts for killing his father. It was a punishment not necessarily dished out by some benevolent deity, but rather by life itself, buried beneath the earth in a hell created for those that did not belong. First, those early settlers, tempted by the dark arts and a curiosity for the macabre, and since then, how many tainted souls had been sent their way, or to any other similar sites around the world? Justin couldn't believe that such survival was only achieved by one group. He had studied enough at school to know there had always been a global obsession with dark magic.

As he took a step in the darkness, he felt his feet catch on something. As large as a rock but too light to be such, he froze, his acceptance of his fate not strong enough to override the fear that it conjured. He knew what lived in the darkness and had seen its destructive power.

He made it into a crouch, ignoring the pleas of his failing body to take it easy. Declan ran his hands over the floor, quickly finding the strange orb he had kicked. Lifting it from the floor, he winced as the pain in his shoulder erupted like a fire, consuming him. He remembered the bite and was momentarily glad for the darkness, for it meant he could not see the savagery of the wound. The orb carried a little weight, which, while substantial, did not fit with the side of the object he held. Much like the small package that arrives in a large box, offering what appears to be nothing but filling.

With his sight taken from him, Declan did the only thing he could think of. He shook the orb, raising it to his ear as he did. There was something inside that sloshed around, adding to the mystery, until suddenly, the thing broke, shattering in his hands, spilling its lukewarm contents over Declan's hands.

Even in the darkness, he knew an egg when he felt one shatter. Something solid landed in the palm of his hands and instantly legs appeared and wrapped around him. Shaking his arms, he tried to dislodge the creature, doing so on the fourth attempt. He heard the body hit with a wet splat. He doubted the impact would be enough to kill whatever it was, but he couldn't spend time worrying about it. Declan knew he needed to move, before whatever it was had the chance to strike again.

He turned back, heading away from the direction he had hurled the creature. He took two steps before stumbling once again, his boot finding another egg, and just beyond it another. His blood chilled as his mind started to multiple the eggs, using the size of the chambers he had seen until that point as a reference. He imagined a sea of eggs, some as large as a small child, each one containing some new beast. His brain painted the eggs in different colors, like horror-filled Easter eggs, faded to a dull pastel by the dark conditions in which they were incubated.

An urgency filled Declan's movements as he tried to find a wall so that he could at least get his bearings.

The first crack rang out in the darkness, echoing like a twig snapping just beyond a tent, bringing a surge of both adrenaline and fear to the child lying away inside. Declan did not even have time to hope it was a singular occurrence before more cracks sounded, coming in such quick succession they sounded like an echo.

The sound of wet limbs, dripping with whatever slime-like substance served as their amniotic fluid made Declan shudder. He could feel their freshly birthed limbs unfurling as if they were all brushing his flesh as they did. It was a sound unlike anything he had heard before, and he hoped it would not be the last thing he would ever hear.

Declan reached a wall, and reached up, desperate to find a way out of the pit. It surprised him to find the wall soft, a depression carved into to the earth rather than the rock.

It was his change. He dug his fingers into the compact earth walls and started to climb, He grunted as he hauled himself out of the earth as if he were digging his way out of his own grave. His body screamed in pain, and he felt the bite wounds tear open, the warm trickle of blood heating his sweat-chilled spine.

He had no reason to believe that he was climbing anywhere, with no way to see what was around him. But Declan thought he could hear something, something beneath the rumbling cracking of eggs.

Several feet up, suddenly Declan's reaching hand found empty space. The wall ended, and his spirits rose. He had made it.

A new urgency drove his body, his tired limbs finding that extra reserve to help push him up. Pain shot through Declan's hand. His fingers were trapped, something was standing on them. Suddenly, hands were grabbing at him, tearing at his hair and flesh. With his body only halfway out, he was unable to fight back as blows rained down on him, clubbing at him in an attempt to drive him back down into the hatchery.

Declan tried to hold on, but ultimately, their assault was too great, and he fell. The few moments he spent in the air, lost in the darkness, held a strange level of tranquility for him, a moment wherein everything was possible.

He had only experienced it once before, and that was in the final few seconds before they opened the prison doors and cast him back out into the world. In those final moments of his incarceration, he was a truly free man. His time was served, and the outside world had yet to judge him. In those moments, as the light appears around the door, like the sun re-appearing after a solar eclipse, anything was possible.

Declan hit the ground, landing on an egg, which shattered beneath his body. His head bounced off the ground, and he could hear the insects scurrying towards him, eager to get the first taste of his meat.

He looked up, into the dark, and thought he saw a light illuminate the ledge he had been thrown from, his mind playing tricks on him. He thought he saw the shapes of three creatures, standing watch over him, making sure he stayed put and allowed their pets to feast.

The first limb reached him, jabbing out inquisitively, poking Declan in the cheek. The hairy leg pushed further, stabbing through the flesh of his face. He cried as he felt others surround him.

His time had come, and while he was not ready, he knew he had no chance of fighting back, and so submitted himself to his fate.

A heavy crash sounded to his left, and Declan felt the creature's attention get drawn to it as if that offering held the promise of a far sweeter meal. Swiping out, Declan brushed two of the things from his chest. He estimated that each was the size of a house cat.

"Declan?" a strained voice called, and suddenly, a light appeared and filled the chamber, the minerals embedded in the rock ceiling catching the light, amplifying it enough for the sea of horror in which Declan was adrift to come into focus.

***

Justin followed the sound of his brother's screams, moving through a tight crack in the rock, passing through the wall into another section of the warren that had been dug into the earth.

He could hear water, and the air was moist and damp. Justin jumped as something dripped onto his head causing Justin to raise his gaze. He was surprised to see that he was no longer in the caves, but rather a tunnel built into the earth. Wooden beams supported the old mine shaft, while roots dangled from the ceiling like exposed nerves. He was deep inside the beast of the mountains now, and there could be no more turning back.

He heard something up ahead of him, hidden in the darkness that the lantern he carried could not touch. The light was comforting, but it also brought with it a level of dread, for its power only extended so far, expanding Justin's range of vision while making him a target for whatever remained hidden in the shroud.

Nervous, he clutched the sword in a white-knuckled grip, the weight of it burning his already-exhausted arms, Justin pushed on. He could hear something up ahead and raised the lantern higher to try and squint into the lurking gloom.

A figure appeared, it's back to him, and then another. Justin was sure there was a third there also, but there was no time to ponder it. His light caught their attention and the creatures turned on him.

One charged forward, moving at a lolloping pace, dragging one leg behind it. The limb appeared to be lacking all joints and dragged uselessly along the ground. The creature was naked, it's body soft and dough-like, covered in a litany of silver scars and open sores, which, at first glance, looked like bullet wounds.

Justin backed up, and adjusted his grip on the sword. He swallowed hard and thrust it forwards. The creature saw it coming but couldn't change direction in time. The blade pierced its throat and burst out of its neck. The thing continued its advance for a few more steps, biting at the sword as if it believed it could eat its way through. Finally, it went limp and fell, pulling Justin forward before the sword slipped free.

Justin turned back to the others, but he saw their attention was directed away from him. He heard Declan growl and then grunt before the dull sound of a heavy impact finished things off. Justin charged at the pair, his bloody sword raised and a war cry building in his chest, Justin cleaved the first head apart, bringing the sword down with enough force to travel through the skull and into the neck.

The weight of the two halves of the split cranium was too much for the creature's rotting body to take and so as each half fell to one side, the flesh peeled away, splitting along the spine and sternum, spilling gouts of black blood to the floor. The thing fell backward, disappearing over the edge and into whatever cavern lay beyond.

With one creature to go, Justin felt more confident than ever, but the swinging club shot from the darkness and hit his thigh, buckling his leg beneath him and sending him to the floor. Opening his mouth to scream, Justin saw the second blow coming and moved just in time, the club catching him on the arm instead of directly in the face. Rolling twice, he forced himself to create some distance between him and his attacker.

With the wall of the shaft for support, Justin tried to stand, but his leg was dead and the creature was on him again. Its hands grabbed at him while hungry teeth snapped close to his face. Pushing back, he shoved the thing backward. Its body was solid and heavy, but it gave Justin a little room to raise the sword he still clutched in one hand. The lantern had fallen to the floor, but its light still gave enough visibility for Justin to watch his target.

The creature charged again. It seemed to regard the sword as a clubbing weapon rather than anything else, for it came straight forward, impaling itself through the chest. A grunt of near surprise escaped its lips as Justin withdrew the blade and with a backhanded strike, as if playing a tennis stroke, Justin sliced the belly of the thing open. The wound parted like a smile, before stretching into a yawn, vomiting a mix of blood and guts to the floor.

The stench was unlike anything Justin could find a description for and made him retch, but he needed to get to his brother.

Justin snatched the lantern from the ground and raised it high, in the hopes of finding Declan.

"Declan?" Justin called, gasping when his brain finally interpreted what stretched out before him.

Even with the help of the mineral reflections in the cave ceiling, the light did not spread its reaches through the entire chamber, but it showed enough. Eggs. Hundreds and hundreds of eggs, some as large as a child, and others that looked like regular bird's eggs, piled high, in rough heaps.

Justin saw the broken shells before he saw his brother, following the train of fractured casings until he came to the mound of feasting bugs.

They moved like a flood, engulfing the body. The only way Justin could tell there was a body underneath was because of the pool of blood that spread out from beneath them.

"Declan," Justin bellowed with a tired roar, dropping to his knees as his final shreds of sanity began to snap.

He could feel them breaking and heard the twang of a breaking guitar string as one by one they gave up, like the final strands of rope holding the heroine in place while the hero desperately tries to make it to her in time.

"I'm sorry, bro," Justin whispered.

"Justin?" The voice took a moment to register through his grief.

Justin looked around, sure he had been hearing things. A ghostly echo of his brother's trapped soul.

"Justin." It came again, and as Justin peered over into the cave, he saw his brother.

Declan stood with his back pressed hard against the wall, trying to keep as far back from the bugs as possible. A large scorpion, whose barbed stinger was curled and ready, weeping thick drops of venom, was surrounded by small variants, as well as more of the cave spiders they had encountered earlier.

To the other side, something screamed as a fight broke out between three freshly hatched insects, each the size of a puppy. They tore at each other with vicious strikes, attacking until all three were dismembered; two dead, and one wounded and dying.

"Declan, hold on, I'll get you out," Justin called, getting to his feet as he looked for a ladder or something that would serve a similar purpose.

His eyes fell on the corpse of the nearest creature. It wouldn't help Declan escape, but it could buy him some time. Justin grabbed the body, and heaved it towards the edge, almost falling in himself as the body caught on a rock, and suddenly shot free.

After changing position, to get better leverage, he pushed the corpse over the edge and watched as bugs swarmed on it like a plague. The sound of their hungry mouths stripping flesh from bone soon echoed, but when some left to feast, others replaced them. Soon, more than before were bearing down on Declan. They had him surrounded, pinned against the wall.

"Get out of here, brother. I got this," Declan said, waving his brother away as he dodged a stinger attack from the scorpion. The pointed tip stuck into the wall, the mud hissing as it injected venom into the hole.

"No, I'm getting you out. Just hold on," Justin called back, looking down each branch of the tunnel, wondering where he could find something.

"There's no time. Get out of here; get back to your family." Declan was as good as pleading with his brother.

"You are my family, the only blood I've got left." Justin felt tears sting his eyes at the thought of losing the brother. They had only just been reunited and the loss nauseated him as it swirled around his exhausted mind.

"Get back to your wife and kids. They love you, man. I'll be fine here." Declan tried to hide the fear in his voice but failed. He was too tired.

"I'm not going back without you. I waited for years to get you back, I'm not letting you become a prisoner again just because of me." Justin's throat closed up, his mouth running dry.

"That's what big brothers are for," Declan said, smiling at Justin. "You have a good life, man. I've got nothing. Toss me something to fight back with and get going."

"Good life? My wife is a drunk, she doesn't want to stop and I can't make her. The kids are getting older and then what, I'll be left with a drunk, and enough money to let her pickle herself with." Justin loved his wife, but he couldn't keep hiding the truth.

"I know, man, but she loves you. She's in pain, so that's all the more reason to get back up there and help her through it." Declan dodged again, but into the path of a cave spider, his hungry pincers raking a chunk of flesh from his thigh, dropping Declan to one knee. "Go!"

Gripping the sword, Justin watched, helpless, as the creatures closed their ranks around his brother. His hand trembled as tears began to fall.

"Go," Declan said one last time, his eyes finding his brother's, locking onto them. It was a moment, but it was all they needed. It said everything they had never said and reiterated everything that had been voiced before. It was cementing their bond, yet severing their ties.

Justin heaved the sword forward, its weight suddenly tripling in his hand. Throwing it through the air, it traveled with the perfect, movie-style arc, landing in Declan's outstretched hand, descending into an immediate swing that severed the inquisitive mandible of the cave spider. Gouts of black blood pumped from the wound and caught the attention of the creatures nearby. Sensing its vulnerability, they descended.

Justin remained where he was for as long as he could, but watching only made it worse. He knew that the Crawleigh natives were coming for them. They would have heard them and either found or felt the trail of bodies and damage they had left behind.

With the burden of guilt spreading through his soul, Justin left the lantern where it was, unable to abandon his brother to darkness also. Justin turned and fled. He could hear grunts and heavy footfalls behind him and knew something was waiting in the darkness. He ran as fast as he could, allowing his memory to guide him through the pitch-black tunnels. He stumbled once when his feet caught on a raised railroad sleeper that supported the mine tracks.

He teetered for a moment, but managed to keep his balance, Justin raced back passed the hanging bodies and their haunting echo of the lost years. He raced into the main chamber where the light of the lanterns cast an eerie glow, giving birth to the hall as he approached it.

He didn't have time to stop and consider if it was still empty because he couldn't afford to stop. He knew that if he did, he would break down and never make it out of the cave alive. He thought of his daughters and of his wife. He used their power in this life to drive his energy into his legs, while the tears of leaving his brother threatened to burn his eyes like acid.

He burst into the lit chamber, and headed straight for the tallest ladder, the one he had started to ascend earlier when something kicked his legs out from under him. He tumbled, hitting the ground hard, his already aching head absorbing a lot of the impact. Pain engulfed his body, radiating through him like a shockwave.

Justin tried to use his momentum to right himself but only succeeded in making it halfway to his feet before careening into a wall. His energy gone, he could do nothing but slip to the ground. His chest heaved from the exertion, while his lungs screamed out for more oxygen than he could ever hope to give them.

When Justin opened his eyes he saw the creature standing before him. Yet even then, he couldn't muster the energy to scream. The creature was old, its face folded in on itself the wrinkles were so heavy. Justin thought that they would find dust from the original founding families buried within the skin folds should anybody unravel the men and go looking for it.

Behind him, holding off at a distance, was a hoard of the creatures, each one armed with some implement or another. Their bodies were deformed, the faces misshapen, the byproducts of years of inbreeding and societal segregation. It was clear that they were waiting for the order to attack, which meant that the man standing before Justin was some kind of leader or elder.

The hand shot out and grabbed Justin by the shirt sleeve. He was surprisingly strong and hauled Justin to his feet effortlessly.

Terror had settled in, and Justin couldn't move. No matter how loud his mind screamed to him, he was frozen in place, as if a spell had been cast upon him. He was helpless as the old man walked around him.

There was something about the man that made him seem more human than the rest. He carried himself with a sturdier posture. Confidence came to Justin's mind as he watched the man circle around him, inspecting him like a piece of livestock up for auction.

The man moved full circle, his eyes squinting as he took in everything he needed to see, appraising Justin for some hidden agenda.

With his circuit completed the man stood, his arms folded, only increasing his human characteristics.

"You are strong," he croaked, in a voice not conditioned to talking for long periods, but clearly still well practiced in the art.

"What?" Justin asked, his voice shaking.

"You are strong. You have fought well. We need fresh blood for the next generation to thrive." The man's voice was lacking in any discernable accent, which made it unusually hard to follow the words.

"Blood? You want to kill me?" Justin asked, finding himself strangely drawn to the idea. His body ached and he could not run anymore.

"No, we wish to breed you." The words hung in the air, and for a moment Justin wondered if what he had heard was true.

"Excuse ... excuse me?" Justin stammered.

"When we were driven from our lands, for the crime of witchcraft, the settlers assumed they had condemned us to our deaths, but there are forces larger than those that roam the earth. The spirits saw to it that we were protected, our families given the chance to survive. What you see here is the beginning. The original families, we live deeper, but even our time is growing short. We must have fresh blood to restore out bloodlines and keep us strong." The man wheezed, growing tired from the exertion of talking.

"No, no," Justin said, willing his feet to move, but every time he felt as if he were about to break free, the old man resettled his gaze and the restraints tightened once more.

"You have no choice. You were sent to us; the spirits saw to it that you survived. You are a warrior. Come with me, and you will spawn a new generation." The man held out his hand, the fingers gnarled and twisted, the joints swollen and bulbous. The skin was grey and lifeless, like that of a corpse.

The extended arm shook with a tremor that could not be controlled, and Justin realized that in spite of the man's power, he was still scared of dying.

Justin felt the power holding him lift, just enough for him to move. He twitched, tempted to move his arm and take the man's hand, when suddenly, it disappeared, falling away from his body to land on the hard cave floor. Black blood spurted from the remaining stump, and the overwhelming odor filled the air. It was like a dirty fishpond on a hot day. It was the scent of death and decay.

Howling like a wounded animal, the man backed up, clutching at his injured arm. He dropped to his knees, the agony overriding any remaining power that the man held in his body.

The sword sliced through the air with a delicate whistle, slicing through the elder's neck, removing the head from its body and sending it arcing towards the back of the cave.

Declan stood holding the sword like a batter holding a pose after hitting a game-winning home run. His body was covered in so much blood it looked like he was painted up for a special night-ops mission. The whites of his eyes burned vividly and bright against the black-shaded backdrop that was his flesh.

He looked at Justin in a strange moment of calm, before the charging storm settled over them.

Justin nodded at his brother, who nodded in return, and then they charged towards the ladder.

Declan dropped the sword and started to climb, as the ring of waiting Crawleigh natives charged, their growls turning into the hoots and hollers of a pack on the hunt. Climbing as fast as he could, Declan ascended the bone ladder, struggling to move through the double step where one of the bone rungs was broken.

He could hear the approaching hoard behind him and felt the ladder tremble in its fixtures as they charged up behind him. He chanced a glance over his shoulder, and was relieved when he saw Justin climbing also, his eyes staring up at his brother. Further back, a sea of grey flesh gave chase, scurrying up the ladders with an agility that defied their appearance. Using all four limbs with equal effectiveness, they rose at a pace, with the early leaders swing clubs in useless attempts at catching their prey.

Declan felt the ladder give, the weight of the pursuing horde pulling it away from the wall. He heard the wall crack as the compact earth yielded to the stress being applied.

Looking up, Declan saw the tunnel they were aiming for. He had no idea where it would lead, but had to hope it was a step closer to escaping. They had come so far.

"Declan, it's falling," Justin called as the ladder pulled further away from the wall.

In reality, it was a small adjustment in pitch, but to the panicked mind, it felt as if they were leaning backward, with their bodies almost perpendicular to the floor below.

"I know, just keep moving," Declan called back.

Something whistled through the air and Declan instinctively tucked his head in, hiding as best he could in such an exposed position.

The spear hit the wall and embedded itself a few feet away from Declan's head. Another followed, and another. Looking back, Declan saw the cavalry had arrived and were doing their part to catch the murderous bastards that were trying to escape.

"Declan!" Justin cried out.

Turning his head, Declan looked down at his brother. A spear had pierced Justin through the shoulder. It was not a deep impact, the projectile hanging loosely from his brother's body.

"Justin!" Declan cried out. "Keep climbing, man, we're almost there."

"They are going to catch us, man," Justin said as the first hungry hand reached him. He jumped up a rung, moving out of their way, but it was a matter of time.

"No, we can make it," Declan said, knowing he was lying. They were too fast, too close to them.

"Go, I got this, brother," Justin said, a strange calm in his voice. The words carried a chilling note of finality, and Declan shuddered as he processed them.

"Don't you dare," he growled as he tried to find a way to turn back and grab Justin.

"It's fine, man, after all, it's what little brothers are for. I love you, brother." Justin smiled up at Declan, his eyes glistening with tears, glinting the same as the minerals that twinkled in the rock above their heads, like stars trapped underground.

Justin fell a short way before hitting the mass of bodies, driving them from the ladder, pulling them with him as he hit the free fall to the floor.

Declan couldn't move. "Justin," he bellowed, unable to look away even as his brother's body hit the floor, exploding as a result of the impact.

The temptation to throw himself to the floor, to follow his brother into the peace of death was a tempting one. Declan let go of the ladder with one hand, allowing his bodyweight to pull the ladder further away from the wall. It would be easy.

A growl brought him back to his senses. Looking up, Declan stared right into the single eye of a particularly deformed native. The thing opened its mouth and bellowed again, the few teeth it had small and pointed. They made Declan think of a shark.

His legs moved while his mind still wanted to stay. The survival instinct buried deep within him rose up to assume control.

He charged up the ladder, with a few of the natives still in pursuit, Declan hauled himself up and into the tunnel opening. Rolling immediately onto his back, he kicked at the ladder sides until they came away from the wall. A few more strikes and he was done. The ladder became fully disconnected from its fittings and fell backward, spilling everybody that was still on it to the cave floor.

"I'm sorry, brother." Even though he knew his brother was dead, an overwhelming sense of guilt took hold of Declan as he thought about abandoning his brother to the cave. "I'll come back."

Alone, and safe, for the time being, Declan fell onto his back, panting, gasping for air as if he had just finished running a marathon. There was no time to rest, however. He needed to get moving.

Hauling himself to his feet, he found he could just about stand in the tunnel, which rose steeply, deepening the burn that was already eating its way through his leg muscles.

Tired, and broken, his shoulder throbbing from the bite wound, and with blood still flowing from the as-of-yet unassessed wounds inflicted by the bugs during his escape from the hatchery, Declan forced himself on. He could hear the rabble behind him and knew it would only be a matter of time before they reached him. They knew the tunnels better than he did and were not being held back by the anchor that was their conscience.

Every step he took, Declan felt Justin slip further from him, further from his life and deeper into his new place in his memories.

Tears came and went, moving in waves, but Declan didn't notice. Everything blended into a blur. So much so that he didn't feel the breeze or the smell of the forest as it hit him.

It was a strange sensation, as the tunnel twisted and opened up into a large cave, as if the earth was yawning, granting him the chance to escape. It was like awakening from a dream, finding yourself in unfamiliar surroundings and uncertain as to whether you are awake or still dreaming, lost or merely confused by the changing state your brain was processing.

It was getting dark, the fading light cutting through the trees with an orange glow, making it look as if Declan was surrounded by fire, the flames of hell coming to engulf him. He paused, wondering with his conscious mind if he had died and the rest of his journey had merely been the passage of his soul, rising to reach the hellish forever he had earned the day he murdered his father.

Declan stumbled as he reached the threshold of the cave, the notion of escape teasing him like a carrot dangled before a stubborn mule. Catching his balance, he looked down and saw two sets of dead eyes staring up towards the heavens. He recognized the faces, even with half of their flesh torn away. Ben and Trevor, the couple they had met the first night of the camping adventure. They had been the ones to tell them the campfire tale of Crawleigh; a spooky story, a legend filled with tales of magic and death as a means to keep children in their tents and discourage anybody from wandering off alone. It had been a tale of fiction, a legend, or so they had thought.

Declan crouched down and looked the two bodies in the eyes. "How much did you know?" he asked, his words thoughtful rather than accusatory. "Rest softly."

Declan bowed his head, and reached out to close their eyes, leaving them to their slumber.

Behind him, something moved, hidden by the darkness of the tunnel. Declan spun around and stared into the dark mass, and for the first time in his life, Declan feared the dark. It was no longer a shroud, but it was a presence, a menacing entity that spread like cancer, eating everything it touched. Sure, it could be beaten back one day at a time, but it was a certain eventuality that one day, darkness would encroach for the final time. It was always the victor in the long war.

He thought he could see something, some form engulfed by the shadow. He could feel them all watching him, but what were they waiting for? He asked himself as he backed away, keeping one eye cast over his shoulder, watching the cave mouth. Was it a trap?

The shadows moved, the sun setting at a visible pace, allowing the darkness to stretch, expanding its reach and tightening its hold. Only tonight was temporary, and Declan was not ready to concede defeat. Not after this. Justin's life was worth more than a few moments of fear.

Then it dawned on him. They were keeping to the dark, waiting for night to fall so they could hunt. His mind sprang back to the first night at camp. Justin had told him about some critter they had heard stalking their campsite. They had heard something later too, from inside the safe confines of their tent. It all came together. They had been hunted from the very beginning and had the bridge not collapsed, then they would have been taken at some other point.

Fueled by the knowledge that the setting sun was giving him a head start but working against him at the same time, Declan made his move. His legs felt as if they had been engulfed in the flames of hell he so feared, as the acid in his muscles burned through everything it touched.

He fled through the woods, ignoring the trails and the snatching branches, thorny arms shooting out to grab at him, attempting to hold him back. Undeterred, Declan pushed on. The darkness fell and he could hear the screams as the Crawleigh flood was let loose onto the world.

He tripped, and stumbled, and ran for short bursts. Declan did everything he could to put as much distance between himself and caves as possible. The one thing he did not do, was look back. He would never look back again. There was no use to fear what was behind you when there was such a wide-open space ahead. The ground changed underfoot, the forest floor growing harder before spilling him onto a road, the winding tarmac looking like a river in the heavy evening light.

The pain ate away at his side, bringing him to a halt. Nausea made him want to vomit, but he forced it down. Declan took a moment to collect himself, resting on his knees to try and fight off the faint that was threatening to claim him. He had no idea where he was, but following the road would lead him somewhere.

Determined not to stop, he followed the twisting and turning tarmac, and even as the cries of the Crawleigh faded into echoes before being absorbed by the night, Declan refused to rest.

His feet burned and it was only then that he realized he had lost one shoe at some point during the whole adventure, the exposed sole reduced to nothing more than a bloody mess. Limping, refusing to allow himself the luxury of stopping, Declan rounded a corner and saw the lights of a town. The road moved along a steady decline bringing him to the outskirts of a town whose name marker he missed. His eyes had locked on the first building he saw. A light burned in the upstairs window, and the closer he got, the more he allowed himself to give in to the lapping waves of relief.

Declan had long since lost the concept of time, but the night was thick and surely turning towards dawn by the time he reached the house. The light still burned and Declan realized what it was: a rectory. The small graveyard appeared to his right, the gravestones rising like bone fragments from the ground.

Declan limped to the door and rang the bell, listening to the musical chime that played out. It sounded wrong; such a building, surrounded by the memories of those that were lost didn't warrant a merry jingle. Declan waited a moment, clinging to the doorframe, which was the only thing holding him on his feet, before ringing again, and then after, a third time.

Just as he considered giving up, Declan heard something, the clink of a lock being moved, followed by another, and then a third. The door started to open, and a friendly face emerged in the crack that the safety chain allowed.

Declan opened his mouth to speak, but as soon as he did, darkness flooded into him, consuming him and dragging him down into the depths of sweet surrender.

CHAPTER FIFTEEN

Declan woke with a fuzzy head, a feeling that spread over his entire body, a drug-induced haze that robbed him of the pain he knew he should feel.

When he looked around the room, he saw bare walls with two crucifixes mounted to them, one a simple cross while the other, larger one had a screaming image of Christ etched into the wood. His face was contorted in agony as the crown of thorns dug into his head, while the polished finished made the wound in his side glisten as if still wet with the blood of the Lord. For the rest, the room was bare. The floor was made of polished boards, and even the bed was a simple wireframe, a solid mattress, and a dark woolen blanket serving as a quilt.

Declan sat up in bed, his body slow to respond to the commands he gave. Taking it slow, he pulled back the covers and swung his legs over the edge of the bed. His foot pounded, pulsing with the beat of his heart.

As he got to his feet, Declan tried to recall what had happened to him. He could remember very little since leaving the caves. He couldn't remember arriving at someone's home. Moving gingerly, he was aware that the throb in his foot would be pain had he not been so full of meds.

The room was only small, and the flooring creaked with every step. Declan was not surprised when the door opened before he reached it and a woman walked in carrying a fresh blanket and some clothes. She saw Declan standing in the middle of the room, as naked as the day he was born, and she screamed, falling to the floor in a faint.

Not wanting to wait for permission, he grabbed his clothes from the floor and got dressed, watching the woman who was starting to stir. He pulled the shirt over his head just as another presence came into the room, an older man, whose face he recognized, his brain playing back a portion of his lost memory. He remembered walking, finding the rectory.

"You, you saved my life," Declan said, the drugs keeping his words dull and his tongue heavy.

The man nodded and walked towards him. "I am glad you are awake. Please, sit down on the bed here."

Declan did as he was told. "We need to call the police. How long have I been here?" The words came faster as his mind cleared.

The man's expression changed as he prepared to give the answer. It was subtle, but Declan noticed it immediately, his body tensing in response.

"It's been four days since you arrived. Your injuries were severe, and we kept you sedated to help ease your pain," the man started, but Declan sprang from the bed.

"Four days ... four days. My brother is out there and you let me sleep for four days?" His outrage was all-consuming, the rush of emotions and memories cane charging at him, hitting his brain with such a force that Declan expected himself to stumble.

"It's alright, son, it's alright. The sheriff and his team are out there right now, looking for others." The man remained sitting on the bed while his female counterpart stood in the corner, leaning against the wall, watching on nervously.

"Listen, um ..."

"Father Michael," the priest replied.

"Listen, Father Michael, I need to get out there, help them find my brother." Declan was insistent, yet the priest remained impassive.

"Son, you have taken quite a beating, and from what you were rambling before we put you under, you had quite a trek once you got out too. Just lie back here and rest. Everything will be fine. The sheriff is a good man. He looks after this town."

Declan refused.

"If you won't take me there, I'll just walk back myself." Declan turned and walked out of the room.

The rectory house was small and neat, the walls largely bare save for a painting here or there. The hallway was carpeted, and it felt soft and delicate beneath Declan's feet. Stumbling down the stairs, he reached a hallway that fed into three rooms; a kitchen area, the main sitting room which was again sparsely decorated with a picture of Jesus above the fireplace, tall candles standing either side of it. A two-seat sofa and moderately sized television provided the main rest and entertainment, while a dark wooden bookcase stood stretching along the wall, filled with volumes that all looked as if they belonged in the reference section of a library rather than a rectory living room.

There was a third room, but the door was closed, a large handled key sitting in the lock. Moving towards it, Declan jumped when Father Michael's hand landed on his shoulder.

"I'll drive you. I don't want you walking out there in your condition. But there is nothing you can do, son. Trust me." There was a kindness in the older man's eyes.

The passage of years had wrinkled the man's face, but there was a youthfulness behind it that shone through. Declan looked at him and nodded, noting the tinge of sadness that lurked behind the steel blue gaze.

"Thank you. I just need to find my brother." Emotion boiled up inside of him.

"I understand," Father Michael said, defeated.

As they got into the car, Declan's stomach started to twist and churn. He didn't want to go back to the caves. He wanted to turn and run as fast as he could, but he owed it to his brother. Justin had saved his life, and he could not let his body remain lost. His family deserved to say goodbye to their father.

Tears stung his eyes as he watched the landscape change through the passenger side window. The woods became thicker and the ground they sat on started to rise. It took twenty minutes in the car before they turned off onto a small side road.

"How do you know where they are?" Declan asked, noting how Father Michael had not once asked for directions.

"The sheriff has been out here for days. He drops by in the evening to give me an update, so that I could tell you if you woke." The answer came naturally, and Declan felt himself ease a little more into the seat. He felt safe with Father Michael on his side, even if the man was twice his age and half his size.

The side road was an unpaved and bumpy affair that shook the suspension of the old car as well as the bones of the people inside it.

It didn't take long before they saw the first car, a sheriff's car, the word emblazoned along the side like a label. A few more vehicles stood gathered around the side of the road a few hundred yards further ahead.

Declan didn't recognize the area, but it had been dark, and he had fled in a straight line, not looking for any road or pathway. His only goal had been to escape.

A group of people stood beyond the cars, half-swallowed by the trees. They had a table set up with coffee and sandwiches spread over it. Declan counted half a dozen men, including the sheriff who stood to one side talking into a comms unit.

"That's the sheriff. I'll introduce you to him, but let me do the talking," Father Michael said, his words carrying an undertone that Declan heard, but did not process.

Nobody batted an eyelid as the car pulled up, clearly used to seeing Father Michael out and around the town. They did all turn when they saw Declan with him, marching towards the sheriff like a man with a greater purpose.

"John, this is Declan," Father Michael began, after tapping the sheriff on the shoulder.

Sheriff John Tucker turned around and smiled. He was a few years younger than the father, but his face was stern, the wear and tear signs of a hard life. His eyes were dark and serious, and the heavy black stubble that covered the lower half of his face only added to his imposing appearance.

"Why did you bring him here, Michael?" The man's voice was as gruff as his exterior suggested.

"He insisted. He wants to help find his brother," Father Michael said, his voice shaking, as if nervous.

"You should be in bed. Don't need nobody making things worse up here," the sheriff growled.

"Making it worse?" Declan asked, outraged and hurt by the man's words.

The sheriff didn't give an answer for his radio burst into life with a loud shock of static. The noise gave way to voices, and while the sheriff turned and walked away, Declan followed him, eager to hear what was going on.

"Son, no," Father Michael began, trying to grab at Declan and pull him back.

Declan was not to be deterred, however, and shook the man's hand away, following the sheriff like a rookie during his first day on the job.

"Sir, sir," the voice crackled over the radio.

"I read you, Jones, what have you got down there?" the sheriff asked, his expression deepening into a scowl when he saw Declan still so close to him.

"It's a bloodbath, sir. There are bodies everywhere," the nervous voice on the other end of the radio said.

"Shit." John glared at Declan, hate the dominant expression. "How many do you reckon?"

"I count at least eight, including Grandad." The words made Declan freeze.

"Grandad?" Declan thought back to the old man who had been talking to Justin, the one he had beheaded before trying to escape.

"Fuck, sweet fuck. Talk to them, tell them I'm handling it. They will have their fresh blood soon, and I'll even make sure there is one or two for the menfolk too." The words chilled Declan who looked over at the sheriff, who returned his gaze with a slow smile.

Declan turned, his heart thundering, his vision darkening as his mind processed what he had heard. The men from the coffee table stood behind him, spread out in a line. Their faces were set with the same stern look as the sheriff, while behind them, Father Michael looked on.

"I'm sorry, son," he said as the men closed in.

Declan tensed, ready to fight once more, but there were too many for him. He dodged the first two blows, but a shot to the kidneys sent him to his knees. The attack didn't stop and blows rained down on him, and with the pain medication out of his system, all Declan could do was howl in agony.

"You almost ruined everything, you little shit," Sheriff Tucker said as he twisted Declan's hands behind his back and tied him with rope.

Declan mumbled something, his face too broken for the words to be discernable, but the sheriff made a good guess.

"Why? That's simple. You always look after your family. The first family has powers, and they make sure our community stays well and prosperous. We all live long and happy lives down there. All we need to do is keep the first family bloodline going strong and we will be rewarded." The sheriff continued speaking as his man hauled Declan to his feet and marched him back to towards the cave entrance.

He recognized the yawning mouth, which no longer looked to be offering him freedom, but rather, it was not stretching in anticipation of the offering coming its way.

The man dropped Declan to the floor, and the sheriff delivered a strong, punt-like kick to the small of Declan's back. His legs shot out in response to the pain and were immediately grabbed and tied.

"We all have too much invested in this to stop now, and you, you little shit, were supposed to just be another meal, but now ... well, boy, you killed my grandpa, so I'm gonna pray that they take their time with you." A series of hoots and grunts rumbled from the darkness, and the sheriff laughed. "Brace yourself, tough guy, this is going to hurt."

Declan heard the men walk away, but his eyes were fixed on the darkness. He could see the shapes standing there, waiting to claim him. He was trapped and helpless. Tears streamed down his face as he thought of his brother and Justin's family. They would never know what had happened to him. Would his little girl grow up thinking their daddy abandoned them? It hurt his heart to think of such suffering.

The first creature emerged from the shadows, quickly followed by another, and another. Hungry hands grabbed Declan, dragging him back into the darkness he had fought so hard to escape. He looked back and saw the sheriff standing in the cave mouth, framed by fang-like rock formations on either side. The man raised a hand and waved, sealing Declan to his fate.

THE END

CHECK OUT OTHER GREAT HORROR NOVELS

MONSTROSITY
by Tim Curran

The Food. It seeped from the ground, a living, gushing, teratogenic nightmare. It contaminated anything that ate it, causing nature to run wild with horrible mutations, creating massive monstrosities that roam the land destroying towns and cities, feeding on livestock and human beings and one another. Now Frank Bowman, an ordinary farmer with no military skills, must get his children to safety. And that will mean a trip through the contaminated zone of monsters, madmen, and The Food itself. Only a fool would attempt it. Or a man with a mission.

THE SQUIRMING
by Jack Hamlyn

You are their hosts

You are their food.

The parasites came out of nowhere, squirming horrors that enslaved the human race. They turned the population into mindless pack animals, psychotic cannibalistic hordes whose only purpose was to feed them.

Now with the human race teetering at the edge of extinction, extermination teams are fighting back, killing off the parasites and their voracious hosts. Taking them out one by one in violent, bloody encounters.

The future of mankind is at stake.

And time is running out.

CHECK OUT OTHER GREAT HORROR NOVELS

BLACK FRIDAY
by Michael Hodges

Jared the kleptomaniac, Chike the unemployed IT guy, Patricia the shopaholic, and Jeff the meth dealer are trapped inside a Chicago supermall on Black Friday. Bridgefield Mall empties during a fire alarm, and most of the shoppers drive off into a strange mist surrounding the mall parking lot. They never return. Chike and his group try calling friends and family, but their smart phones won't work, not even Twitter. As the mist creeps closer, the mall lights flicker and surge. Bulbs shatter and spray glass into the air. Unsettling noises are heard from within the mist, as the meth dealer becomes unhinged and hunts the group within the mall. Cornered by the mist, and hunted from within, Chike and the survivors must fight for their lives while solving the mystery of what happened to Bridgefield Mall. Sometimes, a good sale just isn't worth it.

GRIMWEAVE
by Tim Curran

In the deepest, darkest jungles of Indochina, an ancient evil is waiting in a forgotten, primeval valley. It is patient, monstrous, and bloodthirsty. Perfectly adapted to its hot, steaming environment, it strikes silent and stealthy, it chosen prey: human. Now Michael Spiers, a Marine sniper, the only survivor of a previous encounter with the beast, is going after it again. Against his better judgement, he is made part of a Marine Force Recon team that will hunt it down and destroy it.

The hunters are about to become the hunted.

CHECK OUT OTHER GREAT HORROR NOVELS

DEATH CRAWLERS
by Gerry Griffiths

Worldwide, there are thought to be 8,000 species of centipede, of which, only 3,000 have been scientifically recorded. The venom of Scolopendra gigantea—the largest of the arthropod genus found in the Amazon rainforest—is so potent that it is fatal to small animals and toxic to humans. But when a cargo plane departs the Amazon region and crashes inside a national park in the United States, much larger and deadlier creatures escape the wreckage to roam wild, reproducing at an astounding rate. Entomologist, Frank Travis solicits small town sheriff Wanda Rafferty's help and together they investigate the crash site. But as a rash of gruesome deaths befalls the townsfolk of Prospect, Frank and Wanda will soon discover how vicious and cunning these new breed of predators can be. Meanwhile, Jake and Nora Carver, and another backpacking couple, are venturing up into the mountainous terrain of the park. If only they knew their fun-filled weekend is about to become a living nightmare.

THE PULLER
by Michael Hodges

Matt Kearns has two choices: fight or hide. The creature in the orchard took the rest. Three days ago, he arrived at his favorite place in the world, a remote shack in Michigan's Upper Peninsula. The plan was to mourn his father's death and figure out his life. Now he's fighting for it. An invisible creature has him trapped. Every time Matt tries to flee, he's dragged backwards by an unseen force. Alone and with no hope of rescue, Matt must escape the Puller's reach. But how do you free yourself from something you cannot see?

www.ingramcontent.com/pod-product-compliance
Lightning Source LLC
Chambersburg PA
CBHW032018170626
46807CB00006B/2856